What's the Time of Death, Mr Wolf?

Wyld Enchantment Woods
Cozy Mystery

Kura Jane Carpenter

WUP
Wicked Unicorn Press

Dedication:
To **Meredith** & **Gwynneth Fleury**

~ a true friendship
that's gone to the dogs
in a *greyt* way!

Published by **Wicked Unicorn Press**

National Library of New Zealand Cataloguing-in-Publication Data
What's the time of death, Mr Wolf? / Kura Jane Carpenter
ebook ISBN 978-1-99-117725-4
softcover ISBN 978-1-99-117726-1

MAP OF ELLA'S HOME

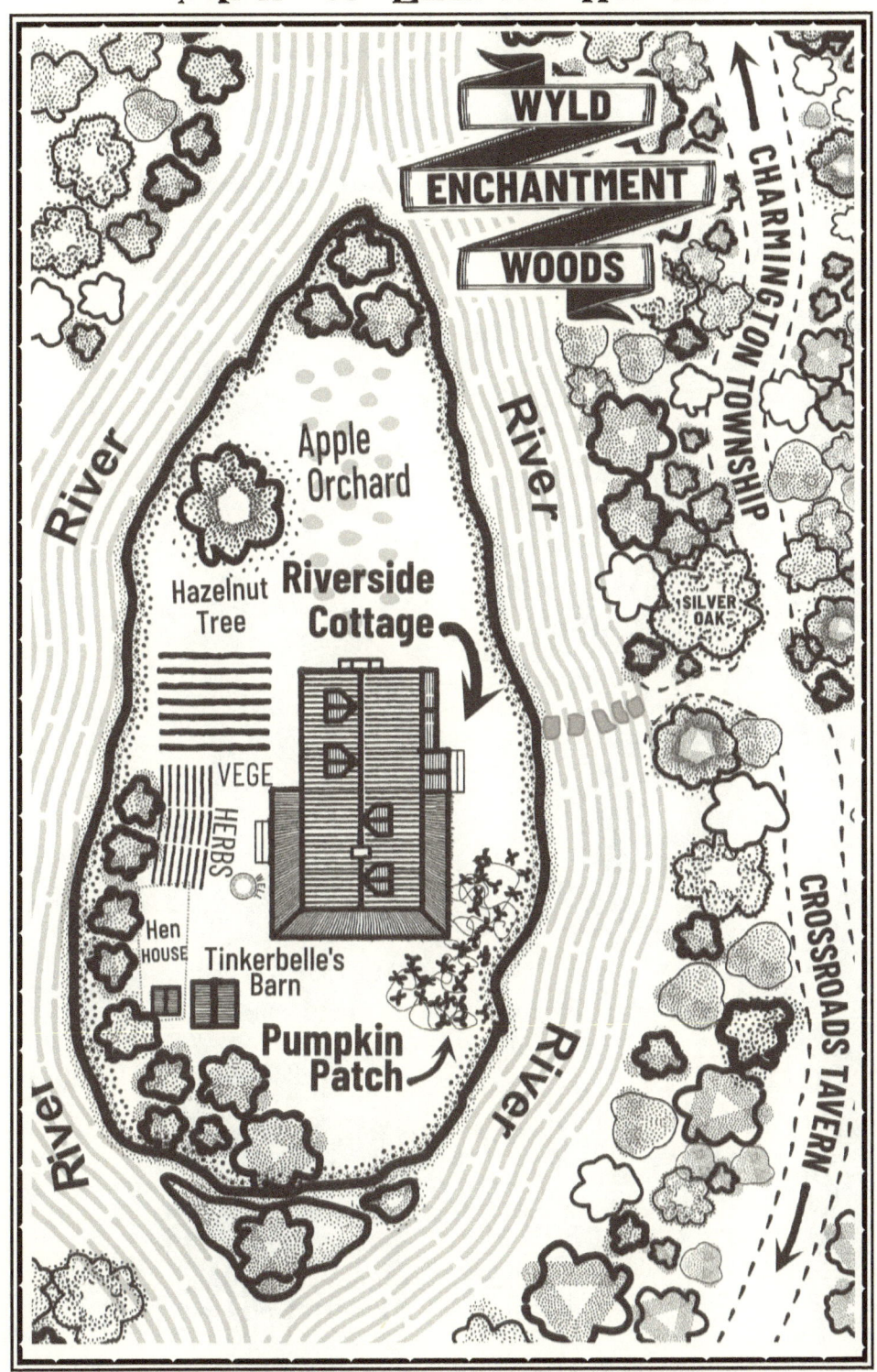

WYLD ENCHANTMENT WOODS

CHARMINGTON TOWNSHIP

River

Apple Orchard

Hazelnut Tree

Riverside Cottage

SILVER OAK

VEGE

HERBS

Hen HOUSE

Tinkerbelle's Barn

Pumpkin Patch

River

CROSSROADS TAVERN

River

River

CONTENTS

Cast of Characters

- **Ella Charming** – Twin sister of Sibylla, sibling of Arabella, Cinderella and Merlin.
- **Tom April** – Rookie Castle Guardsman - Accidentally swapped bodies with Ella's cat.
- Ace – Engineer on the night watch.
- Arabella – One of the Charming siblings, lives in Constantinople.
- Arthur – Proprietor of the Gatehouse Inn.
- Axel Luther – Captain of the Castle guards.
- Baker Street Boys – Orphan children.
- Bron the Baker – Proprietor of Southgate Bakery.
- Cassidy Turpin – head of the night watch – Niece of Dirk.
- Cheapcuts / Chelton Junior – Son of Martha and Chelton.
- Chelton – Butcher – Husband of Martha.
- Cinderella (deceased) – Princess – Sister of Ella and Sibylla.
- Dirk Turpin – Royal coachman – Uncle of Cassidy Turpin.
- Goldilocks – Royal hairdresser.
- Gretel – Millennial – Sister of Hansel.
- Hansel – Millennial – Brother of Gretel.
- Harold Harper – Postmaster – Father of Hillary.
- Hillary Harper – Post office clerk – Daughter of Harold.
- Katie – Barmaid at the Gatehouse Inn.
- Marge – Midwife – A notorious gossip.
- Martha Chelton – Wife of Chelton the butcher.
- Master Spicer – Cook at the Nottingham Home for Unwanted Boys.
- Merlin – Famous Magician – Brother to Ella & Sibylla, lives in Avalon.
- Millie – Haberdashery owner – Twin sister of Sally.
- Mistress Fairweather – Matron of the Baker Street orphanage.
- Mr Beau – Shoe and boot shine man.
- Mr Potts – Travelling tinker.
- Mr Puddles – Willow's pet poodle.
- Mrs Haversham – Former headmistress of the Haversham Academy.
- Nigella Pickford – Actress.
- Peach – Horse – Pulls the royal carriage.
- Perry – Horse – Pulls the royal carriage.
- Prince John – Regent of Sherwood.
- Richard – Woodcutter – Husband of Cinderella.
- Robinne Scarlett – Brewer at the Crossroads Tavern – Daughter of Will.
- Rooster – A Nottingham criminal.
- Rum (deceased) – Former proprietor of the Crossroads Tavern.
- Sally – Haberdashery owner – Twin sister of Millie.
- Sibylla – Queen of Wyld Kingdom – Twin sister of Ella.
- Sisters Grimm – Authors of the popular novel *Cinderella*.
- Tilly – Ella's cat.
- Tinkerbelle – Ella's miniature donkey.
- Tobias – School Master – Aspiring romance novelist.
- Van Helsing – Supernatural Exterminator.
- Will Scarlett – An outlaw – Father of Robinne.
- Willow – Baker – A newcomer to Charmington.
- Wulf – Bodyguard to Prince John.

CHAPTER 1

A Night Out on the Town

Gatehouse Inn, Northgate Square, Charmington.

The evening was late when Ella reached the old stone Gatehouse Inn. The last meal must have been served, the last diner gone, and in the twilight the familiar building exuded an air of stillness and peaceful content. Ella paused on the threshold to knock the snow from her boots and peel off her gloves.

"Arthur?" she called out softly, pushing open the stout wooden door, and then entered the comforting warmth of the main dining room, where she breathed in the lingering scent of hearty meals and fresh bread. She spied the proprietor, Arthur, sitting beside the fire, the embers burned low, his brow pinched, reading a letter. Her friend's expression was fretful. Had he received bad news?

At Ella's feet, Tomcat brushed past her black woollen skirt and darted up to perch on a red velvet chair. His feline face split with a large toothy grin.

Arthur looked up from his letter, eyes glistening, and Ella regretted intruding. In his prime, Arthur had been captain of the castle guards, and though time had altered his stature, he still carried himself with a quiet dignity that Ella respected and admired. "Are you well, my friend?" she said. "I can come back later. My errand is trivial."

Arthur wiped the back of his hand across his eyes. "Mistress, please, come in, come in, it's a joy to see you. Forgive me, I was dwelling on the past." He indicated the letter. "It's been a year already since they informed me of my son's passing."

Ella knew all too well the cruel march of time and touched an unconscious hand to her face and grey hair. But she had not lost a child.

"I'm sorry for your loss," said Tomcat from the chair, his white pointy cat ears dipping.

Arthur gasped and stood upright. "Your cat does talk! Mercy, I convinced myself I had imagined it."

Ella set the willow picnic basket she had been balancing on her hip on a convenient tabletop. "Arthur, I believe you have met Tom April. He's staying with me for a bit until he...recovers."

Recovers wasn't the right word. Tom's injured human body was currently suspended in a kind of magical stasis inside a giant pumpkin in the garden of her cottage.

"Tom April? That's the name of the new guardsman at the castle. I've been wondering why I haven't seen him these past weeks..." Confusion etched on weathered features, Arthur glanced from the cat to the chalk menu board propped up on the bar as if finally having solved a mystery as to why the young man who was becoming a regular hadn't ventured in to try the newest variation of chowder.

"It's me! It really is!" Tomcat grinned, blinking green cat eyes. "I wandered into Ella's pumpkin patch, and there was a shooting star and I accidentally switched bodies with Ella's cat!"

"Gracious, lad!" Arthur looked aghast. "How are you going to transform back? Magic's banned! I mean..."

Ella sighed. "Trust me, we're working on it." She waved a hand. "It's a whole thing..." She shared a look with Arthur, and he just nodded. A simple gesture but one that said, *you can trust me. Always.*

Ban on magic or not, and even if Ella was still in possession of a functioning magic wand, which he was well aware she wasn't, Ella knew that Arthur's loyalty to her was indisputable. She'd known him all his life.

Tomcat tilted his head. "What happened to your son?"

Arthur's expression fell. "It's not the *how* but the *where* that pains me. My boy—to die in Nottingham prison. The shame."

"Arthur, don't blame yourself. Your boy fell in with the wrong crowd. When you ran the guards, there was no finer example you could have set."

Arthur shrugged. No doubt he had examined the past in detail many, many times. "And to think if my son had joined the castle guards, he would now be serving under Axel. Another of my failings! Sometimes, I'm grateful the black fever took my sweet wife—she never had to bear the burden of my mistakes."

"I won't hear you berate yourself over that lowlife, Axel." Ella crossed her arms. "Axel ruined the guards all on his own."

Arthur rubbed his face. "Mistress, take care. Those friends I still have among the guards have said Axel has put out a personal reward for anyone who can capture a talking cat."

Tomcat's hackles rose. "I can't believe I used to look up to him!" His claws extended, piercing the red cushion on the chair.

"Aye, lad, you're not the only one he fooled. A wolf in sheep's clothing, if ever there was."

"And yet my sister Sibylla has rewarded him—have you heard? She's making him sheriff once he's served his time in the lock-up! I can't believe it!"

From somewhere on the street outside, a discordant series of toots and whistles interrupted their conversation.

—toot—parple—toot—squeeeeek!

"Magic preserve! What is that racket?" Ella covered her ears as Arthur went to the nearest window and scowled out between the diamond-shaped panes of glass.

"Just a busker. He's been driving away business all day. I've chased him off twice already." Arthur opened the window, waved his fist and called out, "I'll never sell! You can't drive me out! Off with you, or I'll call the guards!"

"I'll see him off!" Tomcat cried, his fluffy fur bristling. "I'm still a guard, you know."

"Weren't you just told Axel is trying to catch you?" Ella scolded. "You can't let anyone hear you talking anymore."

"That seems dishonest," Tomcat muttered, hunching back down on the seat. "Besides, it's my duty to keep the peace."

"And it's *my* duty to keep you safe," Ella rebutted.

As if sensing this was a sore point between the pair, Arthur closed the window and gestured to the basket Ella had brought. "What have you here? Something I can help you with?"

Ella lifted the cloth to reveal a collection of herbs and spices. "We were hoping, actually, that we could help you. My sister Arabella regularly sends me all sorts of spices from Constantinople. There's more than I could ever use, even if I knew what half of them were."

"Goodness, is that saffron?" Arthur said, picking up a glass jar of the fragrant, orange spice. Peering at the contents, he turned the bottle around in his hand. "This is hard to come by."

"Exactly," began Tomcat. "I used to go with Master Spicer to the market when I was at the Nottingham orphanage and they'd sell saffron for ten silvers a pound."

"Double that here in Charmington," Arthur grumbled, reluctantly setting the bottle back down, "what with the extra transportation costs and deliveries going missing."

"Exactly! Which is why I was thinking you might like to buy any excess Ella doesn't need, say, at half the Nottingham price?"

Arthur had his hand out to shake Tomcat's paw before he had finished speaking, only adding, "If you can keep up a regular supply, I'll pay the full Nottingham price. It's still a bargain."

Ella unpacked the jars onto the table, and after looking them over with great enthusiasm, Arthur agreed to take everything they had brought along.

"See, I told you he would," Tomcat said smugly, his whiskers fanning while Arthur went to fetch money.

"Yes, Tom, you were right. Don't let it go to your head. A broken cluckoo clock is right twice a day..." Ella's eye was caught by something else in the bottom of the woven basket. A slim pink book titled *Cinderella*. "Did you put this in here?"

"I didn't want you to forget!" Tomcat implored, jabbing a paw at the windows. "Book Club is on tonight at the twins' haberdashery. It's just across the square."

Ella glanced out into the twilight and surrounding stone buildings, looking charming with their dusting of snow on slate roofs. "I hadn't forgotten. I wasn't planning on going."

"Don't be grumpy—you'll love it. I worry about you, living all alone in Wyld Enchantment Woods. You should get out more and see your friends."

"Hmm," Ella replied, tight-lipped. She should have known young Tom was up to something when he suggested the late-hour walk to town after dinner.

"Here you go," Arthur said on returning, and he counted the silver coins into Ella's hand.

"Thank you, Arthur, we'll leave you to your evening." Ella scooped up the basket. "And once again, I'm—we're—sorry for your loss."

A FEW MINUTES LATER, STANDING on the steps outside the inn, Ella's breath puffed in the chilly mountain air as she pulled her cloak tight to her throat. She cast a glance up at the darkening sky. If she went to join the book club, it would be very late by the time they had finished. She wasn't averse to trekking home through the woods at night but she hadn't brought a lamp—or even her walking stick. Already her joints were aching. When would she learn?

"I know what you're thinking," Tomcat said at her feet, padding back and forth on the frosty cobbles of the square. "But there's a full moon tonight, not to mention I've checked, and there's a goods barge that leaves Charmington for Nottingham at ten pm. We can catch that as far as the big bend, and then it's just a hop and a skip home."

"Really? Half a mile through the snow is a hop and a skip?" Ella murmured while she clutched the near-empty basket and once again lamented not having brought her stick. "Why exactly are you so keen for me to go and discuss this wretched book with a bunch of old biddies?"

Tomcat sat. He shrugged. A strange gesture to see a cat make. "You seem a bit down. I wanted to cheer you up."

"My mood is nothing for you to be concerned with," Ella replied curtly. She set the basket down and adjusted the ties on her cloak under her chin. In her heart, she admitted she would have liked to confide her troubles, but it was her job to shield young Tom. He had enough to deal with. At barely twenty-three, he should still be able to think the world was full of sunshine and unicorns, but at her age, well into her third century, Ella knew the harsh truth. Innocent people died. People you loved didn't love you back.

Tomcat's little fluffy body sagged and his tail drooped. Ella felt the familiar twinge of regret. How odd to see her beloved cat Tilly and yet know this was no cat but a young, idealistic man trapped inside the cat's body. Would he ever get out?

She took a breath of the cool evening air and pushed her feelings deep down. Hold your head high and carry on. That was Ella's motto. She glanced over at the haberdashery building across the far side of Northgate Square and loosened her cloak string. Tomcat's tail perked up. "We go on one condition."

CHAPTER 2

BOOK CLUBBING WE WILL GO

"**Name it!**" said Tomcat, his fur practically vibrating as he nodded enthusiastically.

"We stick to the story we've told people before. You are a rare Macaw cat, sent to me by my sister Arabella, who works for the sultan in the far-off kingdom of Constantinople, an entirely *non-magical* creature able to mimic a few words. You do not, I repeat, do not, hold conversations or laugh at people's jokes. You show no sign of *understanding*."

Tomcat sighed and rolled his eyes. "Fine, fine, a mimic, not a real boy. I am allowed to eat the finger food though, right?"

Ella cocked her head. "Why would there be any food? This is a book club. An intellectual discussion."

"Oh! Haven't you ever been to a book club? There's gossip and drinking and all sorts of finger food!"

Ah. Now she understood his motivation. Ella tapped a boot toe against the cobbles. "Has this all been a ploy to get away from my cooking? If you don't like eggs on toast every day, you could have just said."

Tomcat ducked his head, appearing more sheepish than feline. "Well...I don't like to complain..."

"Doesn't seem to stop you." Ella glanced over at the stone tower of the town hall and the large cluckoo clock. A quarter of an hour before the eight o'clock start as noted on the book club invitation that Marge the midwife had given Ella a month ago. Still, might as well set off now. A few minutes early wouldn't hurt.

"Remind me again what happens in *Cinderella*?" Ella said, crossing the near-vacant Northgate Square with Tomcat keeping pace at her side. The only other person around was the lamplighter, igniting the infrequent gaslights. Once the whole of Charmington was lit up with row upon row of golden fairy lights. Ella sighed. But with the banning of magic, so too even the street lights must be mundane.

"Ella, you *did* read the book?" Tomcat blinked.

She had not. Why read what she had lived? Cinderella had been her own dear sister. "Lawks, of course, just recap it for me."

"So, there's this amazing ball to help the kingdom's prince find a bride, and all the maidens of the land are invited. And this beautiful, but really poor girl, Cinderella, she's forced to stay behind and do all the housework by her jealous stepsisters—but she goes anyway with the help of her fairy godmother—and the prince falls in love with her, and they live happily ever after! It's so romantic."

"Ha!" Ella replied, her breath puffing an indignant jet of steam. "Wrong, wrong, even more wrong."

"It's not wrong—that's what *happened* in the *book*." Heading for the back entrance of the shop, Tomcat padded toward the alleyway between the abandoned cluckoo shop and the haberdashery.

"Agree to disagree. I don't see how they can claim it's a true story. Fact: Cinderella was already a princess. Fact: she married a woodcutter..." Ella slowed as two small figures appeared from the shadows at the mouth of the alley, their accent-tinged voices raised.

"It's a bad idea, *dummkopf!*" the shorter one, a little girl with cute pigtails, a denim dirndl and yellow duckie boots, said to the taller figure, a blond boy of about twelve.

Ah. Gretel and her brother Hansel. Of course, it was twilight, so they were free to walk around the township now the sun had set.

"I know vhat I am doing!" Hansel replied curtly, hands in lederhosen pockets, his figure slouched. He started on seeing Ella and clutched his chest. "Argh! Highness, you frightened zee stuffing out of me!"

Gretel grimaced up at Ella, little fangs bared in what Ella had learned was Gretel's attempt at a smile. "Oh! Kitty!" The little girl scooped Tomcat off the icy ground and peppered him with kisses, but on catching sight of the book nestled within Ella's otherwise empty basket, Gretel dropped Tomcat and snatched out the copy of *Cinderella*. "I didn't like zee prince. Vhy is he so obsessed with feet?"

"A very good question." Ella could only blink in the half-light. "I shall put that to the twins at Book Club."

Hansel suddenly looked hopeful, as if an idea had occurred. "Can Gretel go viz you to zee book club? I have a task I need to attend to."

"You're not going to see Arthur?" protested Gretel, whacking her brother's arm with the pink volume for added emphasis. "I told you to stay out of it."

"*Nein*," he denied, fending her off, "I have a completely unrelated urgent task. You go viz Highness, and I vill be along shortly." He looked up at Ella, *please, for the sake of my sanity, take her with you!* written all over his smooth and deceptively youthful but very expressive face. "Do you mind?"

"Not at all. I think Gretel would add an...intellectual...element to Book Club." Ella held out her gloved hand for the small girl to take.

Gretel blanched. "You know I'm much older zan you, right?"

"Sorry, force of habit."

"*Danka*, I vill be back shortly, I promise," Hansel called over his shoulder, already hurrying off across the square.

Ella watched him go and then turned to Gretel. "Did I ever ask how you ended up stuck looking like an eight-year-old?"

"Did it involve wishing on a shooting star and magical pumpkins?" Tomcat voiced at her feet, and then gave Ella a look of *Hey! They already know I can talk!* when she scowled at him.

The small girl dug her hands into her pockets and kicked at a patch of snow. "Ugh. Vitch's curse. I hate vitches." She followed Ella into the alleyway. "Next vitch I find, I rip out its throat!"

Chapter 3

Book Club – A Bad Start

The trio were proceeding down the darkened alley in the fading light when a dreadful smell hit Ella and she had to cover her nose. "Magic preserve! What is that odour?"

"Maybe is dead dog?" Gretel muttered, looking around. "Vatch your feets, Kitty." She scooped Tomcat up before he could protest.

A shadow moved beside an iced-over water barrel under a window, and a shabbily dressed man holding a short flute stepped out from the dark.

Arthur's annoying busker, perhaps?

He wore several sheepskins crudely stitched together—definitely the source of the smell. Ella suppressed a gag. Magic preserve! He smelled like a dead wet dog that had rolled in rancid mutton fat.

The busker jabbed a hairy finger from a patched pair of gloves. "Evil! Evil, unnatural abomination!" He set the black pipe to his lips and blew hard.

—toot—parple—toot—

"Get away!" Gretel snarled, clutching Tomcat to her protectively, her sharp white fangs bared. "I hate buskers more zan vitches."

"Devil!" The stinky busker flattened against the wall and cowered from Gretel, but then he locked eyes with Ella. "You are in danger! Werewolves! They live among us!" He dropped something into Ella's basket and made a run for it.

"Learn to play!" Gretel snarled after him. She petted Tomcat's head. "Did the mean man scare Kitty? Kitty is not abomination! Stupid man."

Fearing the worst, Ella grimaced and peered inside her basket, but was relieved to find only a tatty square of cardboard. She fetched it out and squinted to read *Van Helsing. Supernatural Exterminator.*

Light suddenly flooded the alley as a door opened at the back of the haberdashery building. An older woman wearing a rather elaborate pink and green polka-dot gown decorated with crimson bows at the shoulder, elbows and hips, peered out as if to check on the disturbance. But on seeing Ella, the woman's expression lightened, and she beckoned them over to the porch.

Ella clasped the porch railing and climbed the steps up from street level. She smiled, trying to assess whether this was Millie or Sally. Despite knowing the twins their entire lives, she still had trouble deciphering who was who, even though they were fraternal and not identical twins.

"Welcome, Lady Ella, welcome! Sally and I were just wondering if you'd come along to our humble little gathering. We know it is quite a journey for you—and oh, I see you've brought Gretel with you. How...unexpected."

"Hansel will be along to fetch her shortly. You don't mind, do you? She *has* read the book."

"Of course she's welcome," Millie replied graciously, her smile wide but not quite reaching her eyes. "We all know what a special...child...Gretel is."

"You speak like I need babysitter," Gretel mumbled, still holding Tomcat to her, for all the world looking like a sweet little girl with her pet, as she stood on the threshold. "You know I am older zan both of you combined! Millennial means somezing, you know!" She gestured to the doorway where she waited impatiently, tapping the toe of her yellow duckie boots. "Ja, you must invite me in. Rules are rules."

Millie rubbed her neck. "Please, Gretel, do come in."

"Now I enter!" Gretel said theatrically, striding down the hallway. "Point me to zee vine."

Ella closed the door behind her, shutting out the chill of the approaching night. "After you, please," Ella said to her host and followed Millie down the hallway to the large and lace-festooned, lavender-scented backroom of the haberdashery.

The twins had cleared off their broad cutting table, usually covered in scissors, scraps of fabric, and colourful laces, to instead be covered with pencils and paper, several bottles of wine and china plates loaded with little dainty sandwiches. Tomcat was perched on the table and already eyeing the sandwiches.

Sally, Millie's identical twin in fashion if not physical sense, pulled out a chair for Ella to take next to Gretel, who was pouring herself a tall glass of red wine.

Ella interpreted a quick exchange of frantic glances between the elderly twins.

Should the child be drinking wine?
She's not really a child though, is she?
Oh dear. Let's just keep her happy.
Agreed!

"Lady Ella," Sally began warmly, "settle an argument for us. Do you recall that ruggedly handsome bodyguard who was in attendance of Prince John last month at the archery contest?"

The memory of a tall dark man dressed in leathers and exuding a mysterious and dangerous vibe flitted into Ella's mind like a crisp cool glass of iced tea on a long hot summer's day. "Vaguely."

"How would you describe his eyes? Millie swears they were hazel, but I feel chocolate is more accurate."

"You're both wrong, I'm afraid," Ella said as she removed her black woollen cloak and draped it over the back of the chair. "The correct answer is smouldering. His eyes were *smouldering*."

The ladies erupted into giggling, and Ella cast a look at Tomcat. *You wanted to gossip.*

Sally took that moment to tickle Tomcat's chin. "Who's a pretty kitty? Say, '*I love my mummy*'."

"I love sushi," Tomcat said instead, eliciting more laughter.

Millie clapped her hands. "Oh! That's what he first said at Arthur's inn last month."

Sally fetched up a roll of pink ribbon. "You need a smart new bow." Tomcat puffed out his chest and angled his neck so Sally might tie the ribbon more easily. "It's like he understands!"

"It seems like it, but I assure you he never listens to a word I say," Ella muttered under her breath, dropping her gloves into her basket, which she tucked out of the way under the table.

There was a knock on the door, and Ella wondered who else was coming. Marge the midwife perhaps?

"It's probably Willow," Millie said as Sally disappeared back down the hallway. "She's new in town, runs a *patisserie* or something. Just moved here from Nottingham. Her chocolate brownies are divine!"

"I love brownies," said Tomcat mournfully, looking meaningfully at the plates of finger food.

Ella was about to concede to Millie that she could feed Tomcat a treat when barking erupted from the hallway and a little toy poodle with only one ear and trailing a lead burst into the room, chased by Sally and a young woman with vivid orange hair, who, under a bright cloak made of crocheted squares, wore an equally outrageous paisley outfit and more bracelets and amulets than Ella had ever seen outside of a jewellery shop.

"Oh!" Millie and Sally clutched their faces in unison horror as the white dog circled the table, barking and bouncing, trying to nip Tomcat, who yelped and knocked into a wine bottle, which Gretel grabbed before it fell over.

Rocking back in her chair, Gretel put her little yellow duckie boots up on the cutting table. "Vicious beastie! Haha! I like you."

Ella put her boot heel down on the dog's lead. "Yours, I presume," she said, offering the lead of the still-yapping poodle to the woman holding aloft a tray of baking that Ella admitted smelled wonderfully chocolatey.

"Why didn't you leave him at home?" Millie asked, flustered from her usual smooth manners as the dog yanked her guest about in his continued attempts to bite Tomcat.

"Mr Puddles is my familiar," Willow answered, "I'm Wiccan, I never go anywhere without him."

"Viccan? Vhat is viccan? Is zat like vitch?" Gretel narrowed her piercing blue eyes. "I hate vitches."

"Not a vicar, a Wicca. It's a spiritual and ancient connection with the natural environment." The dog yanked her again, and she nearly lost the balance of her tray until Sally also took hold of the lead.

"Ah," Gretel replied dismissively and shared a sceptical glance with Ella as if to say, *I call BS.*

"How about I tie Mr Puddles to the porch railing?" Sally said in a tone that brooked no arguments while winding the lead in close. "He'll be perfectly safe, and I have a nice plush blanket."

"He's very valuable," Willow protested, sweeping her mussed-up hair out of her eyes and setting the tray of brownies on the table. "I rescued him from a horrible man."

"There are no thieves around here. This is a respectable neighbourhood," Sally replied curtly and towed the growling dog out of the room.

"Bye-bye, vicious one." Gretel waved, saluting the one-eared dog with her wine glass.

Millie tapped the side of her nose. "Willow, my dear, you might want to keep all the Wicca talk to yourself—and a select group of trustworthy friends, of course. Magic is banned in Wyld kingdom, didn't you know?"

Willow pushed her various bracelets up her sleeves. "Huh! Another thing my ex-husband didn't inform me of! It's winter here all year round—how is that possible? Sure, I got a bargain for my little shop on Fifth Street, but it's hardly prime foot traffic! He didn't tell me there was a restaurant in the main square—he said *inn*, Gatehouse *Inn*! Does that sound like a café to you? They're hogging all the lunchtime business!"

"I love brownies," Tomcat said, staring directly at Ella with hungry intent in his big green eyes.

"What the goddess?" Willow baulked, doing a double take.

"He is just a mimic, nothing more," Ella explained quickly. "I wouldn't want you to think there's anything *magical* going on. Mostly, he repeats things that I've said frequently."

Tomcat piped up, "My bottom is itchy."

"Oh!" cried Millie, not knowing quite where to look. She bit her lips, attempting to stifle giggles. Gretel made no such attempt and, laughing uproariously, snorted wine out of her nose.

Willow didn't laugh. Just looked Ella dead in the eye and said, "I make a herbal cream that can help with that."

Chapter 4

Book Club – Things Get Worse

"Perhaps we should begin?" Ella said, placing her copy of *Cinderella* on the table on Sally's return.

"Yes, let's," Millie responded, and she and her twin sister hurriedly passed around notepaper and pencils.

Sally clapped her hands. "We're extremely excited to let you ladies know that the publisher of *Cinderella* has heard about our little club and—" she crossed her fingers. "—if they like what we have to say they'll supply us free copies of their upcoming titles for early review!"

Gretel frowned. "I didn't come to be taking notes."

"Sally and I have volunteered to write down the discussion," Millie reassured, "so all we need is for everyone to talk freely, and we'll sort out the rest. And supply the wine."

Gretel shrugged and picked up the bottle. "*Ja*. I'm in."

"I'm sorry, but should that little girl be drinking wine?" Willow voiced. "I know this is the mountains, and things are a little different from the city, but..."

Ella exchanged glances with the twins. What to say? Her generation maintained a code of silence when it came to discussing some of Charmington's more unusual citizens.

Gretel snorted.

"I *prefer* hot chocolate," Ella intoned with meaning, to which Sally and Millie immediately picked up the hint, and the wine and glasses were swept away much to Gretel's disgust, although she rallied somewhat on seeing Millie made her hot chocolate with tiny marshmallows and Gretel set about drowning each marshmallow in the hot liquid.

When they were settled again, Sally sharpened the tip of her pencil and asked, "What were people's overall impressions of the story?"

Ella picked up her copy and studied the back cover, hoping someone else would speak up so she wouldn't have to.

Willow's bracelets crashed and clanged on the tabletop as she moved. "I didn't like the message it sends to young girls." She looked about the room as if seeking agreement. "I'm so tired of stories in which the prince saves the woman. And—"

"That's not what it was about," Millie interrupted, her brow pinched. "It's an allegory on the rewards of hard work." A curt glare from her sister cut Millie short. "Of course, everyone's opinion is valid."

Ella frowned. Did the publishers or whoever only want positive feedback? They had come to the wrong place.

Gretel licked her marshmallow-coated teaspoon. "What kind of man can only identify someone by zeir shoes?"

"A good point." Willow nodded, her movement setting off a jewellery chain reaction of jangles like a human windchime.

"Vho spends zee entire evening with someone and can't remember zeir face? Is *scheisse* if you ask me." Point made, Gretel sat back and slurped her hot chocolate noisily, exposing her little white fangs as she did so.

"She's a vaaa—" Willow slapped her hand across her mouth and stifled a whimper as if having just made a mental connection she wasn't entirely comfortable with.

"What do you think, Lady Ella?" Sally asked, and everyone looked expectantly at her.

Ella glanced at Tomcat whose whiskers fanned out smugly as if to say, *I bet you wished you had read the book now.* "Er...well, perhaps he had poor eyesight or was very short?"

That met with laughter and cries of, "Lady Ella, you're so funny!"

Oooohhowwwowwohoow!

A howl cut through the laughter, and everyone started and looked to the windows and the darkening sky. "Goodness!" Sally exclaimed, attending to the oil lamps and turning them up brighter. "That sounded like it was right outside!"

"A wolf! In town?" Millie clutched a lace handkerchief to her chest, while Willow rifled through her amulets until she found the one she was looking for, a dried-up bundle of heather or something, and kissed it.

"Surely not. Perhaps the echo against the stone buildings is making it sound closer?" Ella suggested. She reached out to pet Tomcat's coat and pat down his hackles.

"Here, everyone, kiss this," Willow said, unlooping the withered plant from about her neck. "It's wolfsbane."

"*Nein!*" Gretel refused, pushing the plant away when Willow thrust it under her nose.

"Oo oh!" Sally pointed to the sideboard where Millie had the hot water urn set up. "What timing—I bought some wolfsbane today! It's in the top right drawer next to the green tea."

Millie fetched out a rather scraggly-looking plant with purple flowers. "Whatever did you buy this for, Sister?"

"An awful smelly man was selling it door to door—he wouldn't go away until I bought some."

"It's lucky you did. Pour some hot water over it and make a tincture," Willow encouraged. "Drink it or dab it to your neck."

"Whatever for?"

"To protect against werewolves."

More laughter peeled out from the ladies, and Ella was thankful not to be the cause this time.

Ooooowwwowwooow!

The ladies all looked at each other and edged their chairs a little bit closer together.

"You don't think...?" Sally began.

"My neighbour's cat was eaten by werewolf mice in Nottingham." Willow stood and looked out at the darkened sky. "Perhaps I should fetch Mr Puddles in."

"There are no werewolves here," Ella reassured, glancing at Tomcat, whose fur had gone all spiky again at the mention of Mr Puddles.

"That's what my neighbour said."

Knock. Knock. Knock.

The ladies gasped. Tomcat sprang up onto a high shelf and peeped out from between two leather hat boxes.

The moment of tension passed. Ella asked Willow to tempt Tomcat down from the shelf with a sandwich, while Millie poured everyone more chocolate and Sally went to answer the door. She returned a moment later with Marge the midwife.

"Sorry I'm late. A stray dog tried to bite me. I gave it a kick, but I ended up having to go the long way around to avoid it," Marge said while removing her red cape and running a hand through her short blond curls. She plonked herself down next to Ella and grinned like anything. "Lady Ella, I am dying to know! Spill the beans on Tom April."

"I'm sorry?" Ella shot a glance at Tomcat, who was now sitting in Willow's lap and daintily eating a large slice of fudge brownie. At least someone was enjoying themselves.

"You told me yourself, just last month! I've asked around, and no one has seen him, so I assume Tom April is still tucked up in your cottage?"

"Oh, what's this?" Sally enquired, raising an eyebrow, and Millie absently stirred her hot chocolate with her pencil. "Young Tom April is *living* with you?"

Gretel elbowed Ella. "Old dogs have many tricks, *ja*?"

"I think it's beautiful. An older woman and a young man as lovers," Willow voiced and then petted Tomcat as he suddenly coughed up brownie.

Ella's lips thinned, but she held her head high. "Contrary to what you may all be thinking, young Tom has been gravely injured." What could she say without giving away Tom's secret? "He is stable but unconscious." That was true of Tom's human form, certainly.

"Has the doctor been to see him?" Millie asked, looking genuinely concerned.

"Zat spoilsport," Gretel responded with a dismissive shake of her pigtails. "Did you know he wrote a book on how to treat poisons? Takes all zee fun out of it."

"Perhaps I could take a look?" Willow piped up. "I've got a new aura cleansing crystal I've been dying to try out."

"Thank you, ladies, but I am quite capable of tending him." Ella looked at Tomcat, who had hunched down, his little ears dipped. "I am sure in time he will recover."

Or he would not. Alas, who could say? Would Tom be stuck forever as a cat? At least hopefully informing people that Tom was injured and recovering at her cottage would help keep his secret. He was new here, didn't have family and with his employer Axel locked up, it was unlikely anyone would come looking for him.

"In the meantime, let us not forget Tom was—*is*—a hard-working, kind young man. I'm sure none of you would allow a bad word spoken against him while he is unable to speak for himself."

"I'm not one to gossip, but—" Marge lowered her voice, and everyone except Ella leaned closer. "—I heard that Axel shot Tom April because they were both fighting over the same woman!"

"How romantic!" Sally exclaimed, thoroughly intrigued. "Who?"

Ella leaned back. "Magic preserve! Can't we respect people's privacy?"

"*Ja*," Gretel agreed, crossing her arms. "Rumours are poison." She cast a sour look at Willow. "Like vitches lies."

"Ginny Bron—the baker's wife!" Marge blurted, her fat little cheeks all aglow.

Ella sighed. One day perhaps Marge might experience the other side and be the victim to wanton rumours rather than the spreader. Then she might learn the error of her ways. Or not.

Millie tutted, and Ella hoped the older woman would back her in refuting any rumours, but instead Millie added, "That's not who I heard, I heard it was—"

Ooooowwwowwooow!

The ladies' conversation ceased, all transfixed by the eerie howl.

At that moment, the oil lamps flickered and one puffed out. The ladies drew even closer together. All waiting to hear if the howl might ring out again.

"Can you imagine," Sally whispered in the low light, "half-man, half-beast..."

"Prowling outside your bedroom window," Marge added with a giggle.

"Good evenink," said a male voice from the shadows.

"Argh!" The ladies collectively shrieked, and Gretel threw an egg sandwich at her brother.

"Gracious!" Millie scolded, standing up to fix the extinguished oil lamp. "Hansel, you scared the daylights out of us!"

"Sorry!" Hansel answered, little hands held up in apology. "I came to fetch Gretel. I did knock. No one came."

Ella narrowed her eyes and looked at Gretel, who was now grinning like she found something vastly amusing. "Why don't *you* need to be invited in?" Ella questioned Hansel. "When Gretel was quite insistent? Rules are rules, she said."

Hansel just blinked. "Vhat rule? Zere is *nein* rule."

The room went deathly quiet. Everyone stared at Gretel.

She burst into laughter. "Vhat? Is funny! Your faces!" Gretel mimed creeping up and down the room. "You all zink you are safe! *Nein*, Gretel cannot creep inside uninvited!"

Despite herself, Ella found she was rubbing her neck just like the others. "Perhaps Gretel has had a little too much wine."

"*Ja*," Hansel said with a brotherly sigh and turned to his little sister. "You vant to go out, you must play nicely."

Ooooowwwwowwooow!

Everyone looked up.

"Oh *ja*, zat reminds me," Hansel said, pointing to the hallway. "Was zere something tied to zee porch railing?"

"What? Mr Puddles is *gone*?" exclaimed Willow in horror and launched herself off down the hall.

"Oh!" Marge wailed, clutching her bare throat. "The wolf must have got him!"

CHAPTER 5

OH DEAR, MR PUDDLES!

"Zank you for looking after Gretel," Hansel said with a formal bow, and then grabbed his sister's hand and towed her outside where Willow could be heard calling for Mr Puddles.

"Oh dear." The haberdashery twins voiced Ella's own concerns as they all made their way out onto the back porch. The blanket and leash were still there, but there was no sign of Mr Puddles. "He can't have gotten far," Millie called out to Willow, who was further down the alley and checking behind some bins.

Sally turned to her sister. "Fetch the lamps. We'll help her look. I feel dreadful. I shouldn't have insisted the dog be put outside."

Ella picked up the lead, still tied to a railing.

"Has it snapped?" Marge enquired while she tied on her red midwives cape.

Ella thumbed the end of the lead. The fibres were frayed and damp. "Chewed through."

"Oh!" Marge wailed. "It was the wolf! Definitely the wolf!" She grabbed a lamp from Millie who had reappeared and called out to Willow, "The wolf, the wolf got Mr Puddles!"

"That's not helpful," Ella called out to Marge as the twin sisters, clutching each other and one lamp between them, followed the midwife down the porch steps. "The dog is missing. Nothing more."

"The wolf got Mr Puddles!" Marge repeated loudly, completely ignoring Ella's caution. She hurried off to join Willow, and the group split into pairs to hunt for the wayward poodle.

Tomcat brushed past Ella's boots and she said quietly to him, "How's your sense of smell?" She held out the chewed lead. "Does this smell like wolf to you?"

"I'm not sure I know what a wolf smells like…" Tomcat replied, but he had a sniff and then poked around and investigated the various items on the porch, including the blanket, the railing, and the steps. "That's interesting. I *can* make out different scents! There's you—you smell like apple pie. There's the blanket, that's lavender, like the twins' haberdashery, there's a hint of carbolic soap…"

"Hmm, the soap will probably be Marge," Ella concluded. "I expect, being a midwife, she's careful about hygiene."

Tomcat stood up on his hind legs and sniffed the air and then went and nosed the steps before repeatedly darting up and down the porch. "I can definitely smell Mr Puddles. But there's something horrible too. Like dead rats. There's so much confusion! Everything is saturated with rancid mutton fat."

"Ah! Just like the busker—did you notice that before? I thought he smelled dreadful." Ella grasped the handrail and ventured down the steps. "Come on, let's see if we can help."

"Do you think the busker stole Mr Puddles?" Tomcat padded down the steps after Ella.

"I don't think anything right now, but it's more likely than a wolf having made it inside the town gates. And Willow did say Mr Puddles was valuable." Ella peered down the alley between the haberdashery and the cluckoo shop. The cluckoo shop had gone out of business. Could Mr Puddles have found a way inside and gotten locked in? She rattled the backdoor. The door opened and she swore under her breath.

"Hey!" Tomcat did a double take. "Should that be unlocked?"

Ella pulled the door shut. "Just a trick of the light. Everything's locked up tight." She moved off down the alleyway, heading to Northgate Square.

"But..." Tomcat began.

"Don't fuss, it's just a little quirk of my natural wyld magic," Ella cut him off. "Please forget what you saw. Come along, Willow needs our support. I'd be frantic if I were in her shoes."

Tomcat didn't reply, but his white fluffy tail flicked in a manner that suggested he definitely planned on asking her later.

Out in Northgate Square, Ella caught up with the other Book Club ladies, who were accosting the few passers-by out this late, though being a Sunday, it was fairly quiet, except for Marge's repeated hollering of "Wolf! A wolf has eaten my friend's dog! Help!"

Sally had an arm around Willow, who had tears streaming down her face. Clearly, the search for Mr Puddles had drawn a blank thus far.

"There, there," Millie was saying, trying to soothe and be the voice of reason against Marge's continuing lack of reason.

"Wolf! Help! Help!" Marge ran around on the spot. Despite failing to actually look for Mr Puddles, her alarmed cries were attracting attention. Lights above shops were flickering on and curtains twitched.

"What is all this racket?" shouted a cloaked person from atop the town wall at the north gate. A lantern illuminated a youthful face that Ella found vaguely familiar. "You're disturbing the peace!"

"That's Cassidy Turpin," Tomcat murmured, brushing back and forth in a very cat-like manner against Ella's boots, like he didn't know he was doing it. "She's one of the night watch guards."

Interesting... Did young Tom have a bit of a crush on Miss Turpin?

"Call yourself a member of the town guard?" Marge retorted, wagging a finger at the younger woman dressed in sturdy leathers against the chilly night air. "You should be down here, helping us search for my best friend's extremely valuable poodle."

"I am coming down," Cassidy replied calmly, passing her lantern to another guardsman and climbing down a wooden ladder set against the town wall. "I'm going to write you a citation. You know how Queen Sibylla feels about rebellious gatherings!"

"How rude," blustered Marge, clasping her short red cape about her dumpy little body, for all the world looking like a plump raspberry-coloured bat or possibly some kind of beetroot dumpling. "Whatever are you talking about? I'm not a rebel!"

I might be, Ella thought and bent down to scoop Tomcat into her arms. Book Club was more entertaining than she had anticipated.

Jumping down from the last step, Cassidy pushed her raven-black fringe out of her eyes and cast an appraising sweep over the gathering. "And yet you're wearing a red cloak." She tutted at Marge. "You know who else is famous for wearing a red cloak? The rebel leader calling himself—or herself—the Red Unicorn. Which means this lot must be your merry band of rebels." She patted a pocket on her leggings and pulled out a pencil and notepad. "Lucky me. Citations all round, and it's barely half nine."

"We're a *private* book club, not a band of ruffians," huffed Marge and the haberdashery twins nodded. Willow, however, seemed to sink into herself, huddling between the older women, as if not wanting to draw any attention. "And I'm a midwife. Midwives wear red capes, everyone knows that."

"Aha! A full confession, is it?" Cassidy flicked through to a blank page. "The Red Unicorn is also the town's midwife? I'm going to lose the guards' pool for not guessing that combo." The young woman's eye caught Ella's and she winked.

Ella found herself warming to this drily spoken young woman who had managed to curtail Marge's incessant cry of "Wolf!" with little more than a school teacher attitude and a pencil, which Ella now noted didn't even have a lead.

"One last question before I lock you all up," Cassidy said, pointing with her broken pencil over towards the Gatehouse Inn. "Is your poodle missing an ear like that one?"

A wave of relief washed over the book club as Mr Puddles trotted up to them, licking his little snoot. He yipped and barked, jumping up against Willow's legs.

Relief was short-lived. Mr Puddles' white muzzle was stained red.

"Mr Puddles, are you hurt?" Willow cried, aghast with dawning horror.

But no. It wasn't Mr Puddles' blood. Little red footprints trailed back to the side entrance into the Gatehouse Inn courtyard.

"Wait here," Cassidy ordered, taking Millie's oil lamp. She followed the trail of blood and disappeared behind the inn.

Peeep! Peep! Peeeep!

Three sharp whistle blows pierced the air, and Tomcat sat up in Ella's arms as Cassidy reappeared, her youthful face pale but resolute, a whistle in her lips. She raised the oil lamp to signal the other guards on the gate.

"Magic preserve!" Ella gasped, hurrying toward the Gatehouse Inn, only to have Cassidy block her path. "My friend Arthur lives there! You have to let me pass!"

Mr Puddles made a break for it, easily side-stepping the guardswoman. "Wait here!" Cassidy commanded the book club members and chased after the poodle into the inn's back courtyard.

Tomcat squirmed from Ella's arms and dropped to the cobbles, disappearing in a flash of white fur. "Come back!" Ella cried, horrified. What had happened? What had Cassidy found?

"I'm not waiting! I have medical training!" Marge exclaimed, elbowing past Ella and the twins. She likewise vanished.

Tomcat returned a few seconds later. His emerald-bright eyes were wide in the darkness. Little pink mouth agape, he panted like he couldn't get the words from his lungs.

"Murder!" screamed Marge from beyond their view. "Murder! Oh! Arthur! He's dead! He's very dead!"

Ella fell to her knees. *Magic preserve! Not Arthur! Please, be wrong!*

"Tom?" Ella whispered as the twins cried out as Willow fainted in their arms. "Tell me she's wrong!"

Tomcat shook his head. Tiny body quivering in the streetlight, eyes glistening with tears. "It's true. Arthur is dead." Tomcat gulped. "His throat...it's been ripped out."

Marge came barrelling back out onto the street shouting, "Mr Puddles has killed Arthur! Bad dog! Very bad dog!"

CHAPTER 6

THE MORNING AFTER THE MURDER

ELLA'S HOME, RIVERSIDE COTTAGE, WYLD ENCHANTMENT WOODS.

Ella didn't often cry. She had been brought up in the public spotlight and had suffered personal tragedy more than once. She knew how to keep her emotions in check. But she cried that night.

The events immediately following the discovery of Arthur's body were little more than a blur, but once she'd returned home and crawled into bed, the tears had flowed.

Dawn came and went. Morning light flooded her attic bedroom and yet she stayed abed. Beyond the dormer window, the sky was bright blue. It would be a mild day, possibly even warm in the afternoon. It was July; theoretically, this should be mid-summer, but the landscape revealed a snow-shrouded forest. Eternal winter reigned in the kingdom of Wyld Enchantment Woods. Once her little cottage had been separated from the forest, having been built on its own tiny island in the middle of the river, but as the river itself had been frozen solid for two decades, could the cottage still be considered an island? Anyone might walk across.

Ella pushed the musing aside. What did it matter? The thought was nothing more than a distraction to occupy her mind while she tried not to dwell on the sadness of last night.

Her friend Arthur was gone.

Ella balled her sodden handkerchief and pulled the covers up to her chin. Maybe she would just lie in today. No one would miss her. Tom would take care of her animals, her donkey Tinkerbelle and the ladies, her flock of chickens. She had no other responsibilities.

As if proving her point, there was a soft knock on the door. A moment later, Tomcat peeped around the door and from seeing her nod, he padded to the foot of the feather bed and said, "I've let Tinkerbelle out of the barn and collected the eggs." He hitched a paw. "I've made you a pot of tea and prepared crumpets, but I can't carry the tea up the stairs without spilling." His shoulders sagged and ears dipped. "Sorry, I tried."

Ella felt a twinge of guilt. Here she was being a useless lump when Tom was upset he couldn't wait on her hand and foot when he had already shown her so much kindness.

"Thank you, Tom, that was very thoughtful. I'll be down shortly." And she added just before he left the room, "I'm glad you're here."

Once dressed and seated at the scrubbed pine table in her snug little kitchen at the back of the cottage, her hands clasped about a ceramic cup of Tom's own devising of herbal tea—ginger, turmeric, and black pepper—Ella felt a little better. She watched as Tomcat, at the woodstove, reached for a jug suspended over the cooktop held aloft by a series of pulleys and levers. He pawed a lever that tilted the jug. Batter poured out onto a waiting pan. Tomcat looked over his shoulder, a wide grin on his feline features.

That was new. The cottage must have grown the device recently.

The entire cottage had been grown from wyld magic, although it had remained unchanged and dormant for the past two decades until the pumpkin patch had taken it upon itself to encase Tom's injured human body inside a giant six-foot pumpkin.

Now little features, the cat flap, the cat-friendly cooking devices, had begun popping up. Clearly, the house approved of Tomcat and wanted to accommodate him, but Ella also felt a growing sense of concern. What if the house never intended to return Tom to his human body?

"How's *your* pumpkin looking?" Ella enquired, assisting Tomcat with the last stage of delivering the crumpet stack to the table and cutting thick slices of butter. "Any signs of ripening?"

"Still green," Tomcat said with a sigh while he waited for Ella to cut his portion into little bite-sized squares. They sat eating in silence. But Tomcat's tail flicked, a sure sign something was on his mind. Ella hoped he'd forgotten about the incident with the locked door last night, and she was relieved when he said, "I need to write a letter." He held up his thumbless paws. "I could use some help."

"It's the least I can do," Ella said immediately, meaning it. She went into her parlour to fetch writing tools and saw her copy of *The Guide to Creatures of Wyld Kingdom,* written by her brother Merlin, opened to the canines section. She trailed her finger through the list of various breeds and their key traits.

"Poodles are retrievers," Tomcat said, approaching from behind. "They're used for duck hunting, but..."

"They don't go around *killing* ducks," Ella finished his thought. "You don't think Mr Puddles attacked Arthur?"

Tomcat tilted his head as if undecided. "It certainly looked like he did. Arthur must have been bending down; there was a spilt bin like he was throwing out food scraps. And..." Tomcat touched a paw to his throat. "The wound looked like a dog bite."

"Could Mr Puddles have been trying to get the leftover scraps?" Ella recalled the poodle's aggression toward Tomcat on the cutting table. The dog certainly had shown every intention of wanting to eat Tomcat, but dogs chasing cats was very different behaviour to dogs attacking people doing them no harm. And she knew Arthur. He would not hurt a dog. Although... Perhaps he had been startled. Thought he was being attacked?

"I'm sure Miss Turpin will look over the accident properly, before making any conclusions. She seemed competent," Ella voiced. "If it must have occurred, let's at least be grateful it wasn't under the watch of Axel's dayshift. He wouldn't prioritise it even if a note claiming responsibility had been pinned to Arthur's shirt." She collected her dip-pens, ink and writing paper and headed back into the kitchen, where the warmth from the stove and the pleasant scent of cooking was more comforting than the cold front parlour that looked out onto the masses of pumpkin vines in which Tom's own body lay entombed.

"Now, you dictate, and I'll write," Ella said, shaking her bottle of ink and then dipping a pen into the vivid liquid.

"Your ink is purple," Tomcat said, standing up on the table and peering into the glass bottle.

"Not how I start a letter," Ella said, but then explained, "I thought it added a certain flair. And besides, it was cheap. Now, begin."

"Dear Master Spicer, I really hope you and the other boys at the Nottingham Unwanted Boys' Home are well—"

"Excuse me?" Ella blurted, stopping mid-sentence, her nib blotting the parchment. "The Nottingham *what* home?"

Tomcat hunched. "That's what the orphanage is called." His ears dipped. "It's not very nice, is it? I always used to be so ashamed, but Master Spicer told me, a man is judged by his actions, not his titles. A prince with a wicked heart is not equal to an orphan with a kind one."

"Well," responded Ella, not sure what else to say, "I shall certainly have a stern word with Prince John if I get the chance—calling poor little children *unwanted* when it's no fault of their own they ended up there. Gracious! I am quite incensed. Please, carry on."

"Ahem. ...are well. I'm sorry I haven't written sooner. I have had a...small accident, but please don't worry, a kind lady is looking after me, and I'm sure I'll be back on my two feet in no time. In the meantime, please find enclosed—hold on!" Tomcat leapt off the table and returned a few seconds later carrying in his teeth his money pouch that had been stored on the sideboard along with all his other worldly possessions that the pumpkins had frisked from his pockets before cocooning his injured body just over a month ago.

He placed the purse on the table in front of Ella. "Can you please count it all out, and just keep enough aside to pay for my board here, for maybe, what do you think? Will my body be healed in the next two weeks?"

Ella couldn't meet his eye while she counted the money. To think only a few weeks ago she'd been so petty about her finances and only concerned that Tomcat would eat her out of house and home and here he was, not only sending every spare coin back to the orphanage that raised him but taking care of her as much, if not more, than she had taken of him. Her mother would be ashamed of her.

Ella stood up. "Let's not forget your earnings from yesterday..." she said, retrieving her black woollen cloak hanging on the drying rack above the stove and then feeling around in the pockets, which she'd forgotten to empty in the haze of last night. The silver coins were warm in her hand. She remembered how they felt as Arthur counted them into her palm and she blinked rapidly as fresh tears threatened her composure. "Lawks, I must have dislodged some soot from the chimney," she fibbed to hide her tearing eyes.

"But that's your money, Ella," Tomcat protested, batting her hand away when she added the half dozen silvers to his pile. "You need it. Especially now..."

Ella caught his eye. She hadn't thought of that, but with Arthur gone there would be no more selling spices to him to help earn money to donate to the Cinderella Charity Animal Sanctuary. She shook her head. "You earned the money, Tom. It didn't even occur to me to do something with the spices. Arabella's gifts would have completely gone to waste if not for you. Let me do this. I want to thank the man who raised you so well."

Tomcat touched the back of Ella's wrinkled hand with his small paw and she burst into tears crying, "Soot! So much soot!"

CHAPTER 7

POST OFFICE POLITICS

POST OFFICE, NORTHGATE SQUARE, CHARMINGTON.

Ella set Tomcat down on the ledge of the square's frozen-over water feature. Three orphan children wearing matching stripey blue and yellow jumpers were pushing bars of soap carved into crude boats around and around the statue of a rearing unicorn at the fountain's centre. Much to the children's delight, Tomcat joined in their game of batting the little soap boats back and forth across the ice.

Ella watched for a moment while leaning on her walking stick and then glanced across the square at the Gatehouse Inn. A guardsman stood outside, asleep, somehow propped up-right on his pike. How could Arthur be gone? It was so unfair.

"Are you happy to wait out here?" she asked quietly. Tomcat nodded, and so Ella left him to play and headed over to the post office.

Located directly beside the town hall, the post office had a prime position in Northgate Square. Ella usually avoided going there in case she bumped into Harold Harper, the self-important postmaster, who had a misguided crush on Ella many years ago. Harold had resented being publicly turned down and had made things awkward between them ever since.

Entering the bustling post office, Ella got a lungful of lemon-scented wood polish as she joined a queue. In front of her, the new school teacher, who she had last seen only a few weeks ago at the Gatehouse Inn, was rifling through a large stack of papers and muttering under his breath as he scanned the documents.

Ella overheard the words 'tender embrace' and, by using her stick for balance and standing up on tiptoes, she spied over his shoulder the line *Nay, she cried breathlessly, clutching his strong but gentle arms, our families will never agree to our marriage! We must run away tonight!*

Magic preserve! Was the young man writing a romance novel? Perhaps she should mention the book club to him. Ella sighed. Her thoughts returned to the tragedy the day before just as Marge the midwife joined the queue behind Ella and burst out, "Oh gracious,

Lady Ella, you look as bad as I feel—I didn't get a wink of sleep. Did you?"

Ella thinned her lips. "No, quite." Her thoughts shifted to another who had probably had a poor night's rest. Willow. No doubt she was suffering greatly. Ella wondered how many people the lass had to support her, as she was a newcomer. She recalled that Marge, too, had originally come from Nottingham. "Did you know Willow before she moved here? Were you acquainted with her in Nottingham?"

"Barely, and I'm sorry I do now—what with her monstrous dog," Marge uttered in lip-curled disgust. "She said it herself—what happened to her neighbour—her neighbour's cat probably passed the were-infection on to Mr Puddles, and now none of us are safe in our beds!"

Ella blinked. "Is that possible? Pass the were-infection on?" Magic preserve! What a horrible thought.

"Willow ought to be locked up, if you ask me. Just as much her fault as the dog's. It's a blessing in disguise that poor Arthur didn't survive," Marge ranted, "or he, too, would bear the shapeshifter's curse. Forever doomed to walk alone."

"We can't assume—" Ella began and then stepped back as the school teacher spun about.

"Arthur? What happened to him?"

"Dog attack," Marge replied, angling her head to bare her throat. "Ripped out his voice box, could not cry out. Bled to death."

"Next!" the petite young woman with a pixie haircut at the postal counter called sharply.

The teacher started, and some of his pages floated to the floorboards. Ella clutched her walking stick, loath to bend on account of the pain in her knees, but Marge swooped in to assist, eyes lighting up as she scanned the text. "Oh ho! What's this then, Master Tobias?"

"It's not what you think!" Tobias blushed, hurriedly bending to pick up the other stray sheets as the postal worker dinged her bell impatiently.

"Next, *please!*"

"Well, it looks like you're writing a romance!" Marge grinned and nudged Ella as she handed the page back to its very embarrassed owner, who stuttered something unintelligible and handed the sheaf of papers over to the young lady at the counter, his cheeks now as bright as his ginger hair. "Fancy that, Lady Ella—maybe Master Tobias is the secret author of *Cinderella*? Katie the milkmaid was telling me, rumour has it they live locally."

Tobias raised a hand, both trying to deflect Marge's teasing while answering the questions of the dark-haired girl at the counter, who was increasingly becoming more curt. "We ask that you be entirely prepared *before* approaching the counter," she scolded Tobias while weighing the sheaf of papers. "Time is precious."

"Miss Harper, don't rush him on our account," Marge said from behind Ella. "A writer in our midst! How glamorous."

Miss Harper? Could she be Harold's daughter? Ella looked around, trying to spy if Harold was lurking in one of the adjoining offices. With any luck, today was his day off.

The efficient young woman behind the counter certainly sounded like Harold. He'd wasted no time in getting married when Ella turned him down—engaged by the end of the week, if Ella's memory served.

"Are you going to write a sequel?" Marge continued needling. "You should write about pirates! He's a dashing pirate captain, and she, a buxom—"

"I *didn't* write *Cinderella*," Tobias denied, fumbling to count out his money and pay for his parcel.

"Course not." Marge winked. "Secret's safe with us." She nodded at Ella in a conspiratorial fashion.

Ella doubted any secret was safe with Marge.

"Next, please," Miss Harper called as Tobias nodded *good day* to Ella and Marge and made his exit. Poor lad.

Ella freed the letter she'd penned for Tom from her cloak pocket. "Postage to Nottingham, thank you." The letter clinked as she placed the envelope on the polished counter.

Miss Harper frowned. Her smooth youthful face was marred by the creased brow. "Is there money in here?"

"Yes. Is that a problem? I'm posting on behalf of Tom April. He's sending his wages to help his fellow orphans because that's the sort of thoughtful young man he is." It wasn't like Ella to air people's private business in public, but if there was a chance to counter the foolish rumours floating around, she'd take it, and Marge spread gossip like flies spread disease.

Miss Harper's annoyed expression softened into one of genuine concern, and she reached out and placed her surprisingly cold hands over the top of Ella's. "Oh! Good mother Ella—I heard Tom had been injured!"

"Are you a friend of his?" Ella was slightly taken aback by the brusque young lady's sudden enthusiasm.

She nodded. "I should think so! Does he talk of me?"

"Ah…" Ella struggled to recall if Tom had ever mentioned her. "He's unconscious most of the time, poor lad. Did I forget to mention that?" She hoped this would be an end to it.

"Perhaps I could visit. Maybe read to him? A friendly voice might rally him from his coma!"

Oh dear! The lass was quite persistent. Did she have feelings for the boy? "I'm not sure that—"

"What's the hold-up, Hillary?" a male voice interrupted.

Ah. Harold Harper. Ella's luck had run out.

Walking up to the counter, Harold drew a gold pocket watch from his waistcoat and flicked the watch cover open. "Three minutes per customer, that is the regulation."

"Sorry, Dad," Hillary mumbled, releasing her cold hands from Ella's.

"Sorry, *Postmaster*," Harold corrected, "not *Dad* when we're at work." His hair was a peculiar shade of flat brown that Ella suspected couldn't be natural, considering he must be past fifty. "We must maintain proper procedures…" He picked up Tom's wages-filled envelope and tutted, casting a look of disdain at Ella while somehow avoiding eye contact. "Have you informed this customer that posting money is against policy?"

This *customer*? He wasn't even going to acknowledge her name. Well, that suited Ella just fine, thank *you* very much!

"I was about to," Hillary responded, eyes downcast, tucking strands of her neat bob behind an ear and half-heartedly pointing to a notice on the wall that proclaimed Prohibited Items included: *valuables, flammables and magicals.*

"Posting money makes the service a target for thieves," Harold launched into his own explanation, smoothing his cravat across his chest and pulling down on the hem of his bland grey waistcoat.

"Perhaps you shouldn't have fired Hansel and Gretel," Marge piped up at Ella's back. "Katie told me no one dared attack the stagecoach with those two millennials aboard."

For once, Ella found herself agreeing with the outspoken midwife.

"We must move with the times," Harold replied, fiddling with a shiny brass button. "The stagecoach is antiquated compared to the speed and reliability of the ice barges."

"Harumph," murmured Ella to herself. "If you can't post what you need to post, why does it matter if it *theoretically* gets there faster?"

Harold flipped his pocket watch open again. "Ten minutes, Hillary. Deduct it from your lunch hour." And he strode off into his office, pausing to buff the brass nameplate on the door.

Ugh. Pompous man.

"I beg pardon, Miss Harper." Ella collected Tom's letter from off the counter. "I will pass on your kind regards to Tom when he recovers."

Turning, she nodded *good day* to Marge, and tucking the letter safely into her cloak pocket, she made her way out of the building. Despite having failed in her errand, Marge's conversation had planted the seed of an idea. She'd go chat to Hansel and Gretel and see if they'd personally deliver the letter the next time they drove their stagecoach to Nottingham.

She imagined the look on a prospective highwayman's face, attempting to hold up the coach, only to find the brother and sister smiling down upon them, razor-sharp fangs bared. Marge was right. Who safer? Why, if anyone dared rob them, Hansel or Gretel could rip a would-be highwayman's throat out.

CHAPTER 8

VAN HELSING, HARBINGER OF DOOM

Ella stopped in her tracks. So struck by the horrifying thought, she barely noticed a crowd was gathering around the unicorn fountain where she'd left Tom. She stood transfixed outside the post office, turning the troubling notion over in her mind.

Certainly, it was true that Hansel and Gretel were quite capable of ripping out the throat of whoever they chose, but it wasn't as if they made a *habit* of it... No, and the possibility that either would deliberately harm a Charmington resident was ludicrous—more than that, it was uncharitable mean-minded thinking. She squashed the notion deep down. Why, she herself when she was in possession of her powers, could have created mayhem and havoc with a flick of her wand, and did she? Of course not.

Another thought occurred. Did Hansel go and talk with Arthur last night? She had heard Hansel and Gretel arguing about something to do with Arthur. Perhaps Hansel was the last person who spoke to Arthur?

Ella glanced over to where the sleeping guardsman was slouched outside the Gatehouse Inn. Why exactly did the building remain quartered off? That seemed to suggest Miss Cassidy Turpin wasn't entirely convinced by the poodle-shaped evidence presented last night.

"Danger! Abomination! Heed my warning before it's too late!"

Ella blinked and refocused on the world around her. Magic preserve! A crowd of residents had formed around the fountain. Oh no! What had Tomcat gone and done now? Ella gripped her walking stick and strode over the cobbles towards the gathering townspeople.

Standing on the lip of the fountain, raised a head above the onlookers, the shabbily dressed busker she'd encountered last night was shouting and ranting, filling the chilly air with his booming voice.

What was his name? Van Helsing, yes, that was it.

"Good people of Charmington," the busker cried, waving his hands, "you are in terrible danger! A werewolf stalks this town!"

This elicited gasps from some and laughs from others.

Ella elbowed her way through to the front of the spectators at the foot of the fountain. There was no sign of the children or Tomcat. Thank goodness, he must have had the sense to leave when the lunatic busker appeared. Or perhaps had been driven away by the horrendous smell? Ella clutched her palm across her nose. Gracious, she'd forgotten about the odour coming off his crude jerkin of rotting sheepskins. It was like a physical presence. A wall of stink. Could he not smell it?

"Who are you, anyway?" Tobias the school teacher called out from the onlookers.

The busker rattled a bone necklace that appeared to be made from dozens of rat skulls. "I am Van Helsing, supernatural exterminator and harbinger of doom!"

"You're crazy!" a sceptical townsperson retorted. "That's who you are!"

Ella found herself agreeing. She scanned the ground for Tomcat between people's feet and the items they had set down. Where had he gone off to?

"Crazy, am I?" Van Helsing drew out a ragged copy of the *Nottingham Times* newspaper from last month with 'Werewolves Rampage' across the front page. "Don't let Charmington suffer the fate of Nottingham!"

There were murmurings within the gathering. A few people nodded, but someone else replied, "Nottingham's *miles* away!" This elicited more nods and similar responses of, "Magic is banned here! We're safe."

"Safe?" Van Helsing rolled his eyes. "Ha! Do you think evil cares if it is welcome or not?" He pointed to the Gatehouse Inn. "You cannot reason with a werewolf when its red eyes bear down on you, when its teeth pierce your flesh and drink your blood!"

People were glancing over to the inn now, sharing worried looks and a few rubbed their throats. No doubt, word of Arthur's unfortunate accident had spread like wildfire.

"But...I heard it was a dog attack?" Tobias voiced, sounding a little less sceptical.

"That's right, and they have the dog in custody—saw it myself," another claimed. "Big fierce brute."

"Ha! Do not be fooled by the night watch's attempt to cover this up!" Van Helsing rattled his revolting rat skull necklace again. "Who here has been bitten? Speak up! One among you is cursed! Once the infection takes hold, even the gentlest of men or placid beast is turned wild with uncontrollable savagery!" He pointed to the sky. "The full moon compels, tonight the werewolf will strike again!"

Ella turned to go. She wouldn't stand around and hear this crazy man spreading foolish rumours any longer. "Weak-minded nonsense," she muttered. Extracting herself from the crowd, she spied the royal coach hitched up outside the town hall. And who should be standing up on his hind legs and patting one of the horses, but Tomcat?

At Ella's back, she heard Tobias say in a worried voice, "Wasn't Baker Bron bit by a wolf last month?"

CHAPTER 9

THE COACH AND THE COINCIDENCE

TOWN HALL STEPS, NORTHGATE SQUARE, CHARMINGTON.

The royal coach was, in Ella's opinion, an unnecessarily gaudy object. But then again, perhaps that was the point. More than just a practical form of transportation, it was also a symbol to the world: *Behold, here comes the queen. Get out of the way!*

All carved oak, gilded with gold, and painted in the royal Charming purple, it was drawn by two white horses, their harness in black leather with silver bells, and upon their heads, ostrich plumes dyed a vivid purple.

Yes. Gaudy was an understatement.

Tomcat was patting the velvety nose of one of those horses. "This one is called Perry," he told Ella, "and that mare is Peach."

"Did Dirk tell you that?" she asked, worried that perhaps Tom had been speaking to the coachman. Dirk Turpin seemed a trustworthy fellow, but he worked directly for the queen, who would be glad of any information that might force Ella to do Sibylla's bidding, such as having a talking cat when magic was banned.

Ella took off a glove and scratched the neck of Peach. The creature blinked its large eyes at her and nuzzled her hand. Huffing warm breath across her fingers. When she'd last lived at the castle, some twenty years ago now, the two main carriage horses had been called Cherry and Cobbler. Could these two be their offspring? Dirk might know. She looked about for the coachman, but there was no sign of him. Perhaps he was inside the town hall with Sibylla.

Tomcat's tail flicked. "Don't worry, I wasn't talking to anyone. I just listened to what the children said. When the carriage rolled up, they all came over to pat the horses until the queen shooed them off."

That would be right. Sibylla wouldn't want sticky little hands smearing the brightly polished harness gear.

"I'm afraid I couldn't post your money," Ella said while rubbing Peach's long pointy ears. The mare's large brown eyes reminded her of the pony she had as a small girl. Tomcat looked up. "Turns out posting valuables is prohibited. To discourage thefts and hold-ups."

"I should have thought of that." He sounded forlorn. "But how can I get the wages to the orphans now?" He gestured to his furry body. "It's not like I can travel to Nottingham and deliver it myself, looking like this."

"Where's the orphanage located? Is it far from the coaching post in Nottingham? I was thinking since Hansel and Gretel drive the stagecoach to Nottingham, maybe they could deliver your letter to Master Spicer personally."

Tomcat's whiskers fanned. "That's a great idea! Do you think they'd mind?"

Ella shrugged. "We can only ask." She glanced back over at the increasingly heated exchange of opinions at the unicorn fountain and the raised voices arguing whether Bron the Baker could possibly be a werewolf. Ella tutted. Any moment now, they'd be forming an orderly line and handing out the pitchforks.

Something else across the far side of the square, over at Arthur's business, caught her eye. The jewellery-bedecked newcomer she'd met last night at the book club, Willow, the one who owned Mr Puddles, was lugging some kind of signage board out in front of the steps of the closed Gatehouse Inn. "Tom, how's your eyesight? Can you make out the words on Willow's board from here?"

Tomcat peered this way and that. "Lift me up. I can't see through all the legs." Ella did as he bid. "Oh! It says, 'Fresh home baking—muffins, scones, soups—Fifth Street bakery.'"

"Magic preserve!" Ella responded. "The nerve of that woman. Arthur isn't even cold in his grave, and she's stealing his business."

"It does seem *a little* unfeeling," Tomcat murmured, ever the diplomat, "but she was saying last night her business isn't doing well. Maybe, in her mind, she's just making the best of a bad situation?"

"Best of a bad situation?" Ella was incensed. "Far be it from me to criticise, but that *bad situation* is entirely her doing—Mr Puddles was the culprit! I might go and give her a piece of friendly advice before someone throws a rock through her window."

"Good afternoon, ma'am," a male voice said in a low respectful tone at Ella's back, and she turned to see Dirk Turpin, the royal coachman, approaching down the stone steps of the town hall in his smart purple frock coat. He doffed his black tricorn, revealing an old-fashioned black wig with a ponytail, and clutched the hat to his breastbone. "If I might offer my sympathy, Cassidy told me you were there last night. Terrible business. A tragic loss."

"Thank you, Dirk." Ella shaded her eyes in the bright noonday sun. Was Cassidy Turpin related to Dirk? She'd be about the right age to be his child. "And I am sorry for what poor Cassidy had to witness. Is she your daughter?"

The coachman placed his tricorn back on his head and adjusted the curled raven black wig that was also part of his uniform. "My niece, actually, my sister's daughter, mercy rest her soul. A victim of the black fever, like so many that summer."

Ella nodded, her thoughts returning to Arthur, who had likewise lost his wife due to that same fever. Poor Arthur, to lose his wife to fever, his son to then die in prison, and now he himself had died in such a dreadful way. Life could be very unjust.

She frowned. Across the square, Willow had a picnic basket and was handing out what appeared to be baked goods to passers-by loitering near the inn.

Selling from Arthur's own doorstep! Did the woman have no shame? To profit from the death of the man who would be alive today, but for her dog.

"Cassidy seems a capable young woman," Ella began, watching as Willow in the distance waved her hands as if giving directions to the people she passed out her pastries to. "She's sure the poodle did it?"

Dirk stroked the muzzles of his horses. "Can't say, ma'am."

Ella nodded thoughtfully. "I'm sure Cassidy would have gone to Hansel if there was any doubt?" If anyone was a bite expert, it was Hansel.

"Quite so." Dirk let out a long breath. "And to think poor Arthur was soon to be retired and enjoying his days on some tropical shore."

"I'm sorry?" Ella looked up. "Arthur, retire?"

"Aye, he told me himself just a few weeks back, before the archery contest, said he'd sold up—was looking forward to having someone else serve him drinks for a change."

"What?" Ella baulked. "That can't be right." Had Arthur mentioned anything about selling up last night? No. Surely not. That business was his life. "He wouldn't leave without telling me."

Dirk turned away and fussed with the horse's bridle. "Perhaps I'm wrong."

Over at the fountain, Van Helsing was now doing a swift trade in something. Some plants, perhaps wolfsbane. Ella narrowed her eyes. Two newcomers, both profiting from Arthur's death. That was an odd coincidence.

Van Helsing's claim there was a werewolf hidden in the town made an odd kind of sense. Fear meant he could sell his scraggly pieces of wolfsbane. But as for Willow...

Willow had claimed Mr Puddles was valuable. Why?

CHAPTER 10

A PROMISE MADE

Bidding the coachman a good day, and with Tomcat tucked under one arm and her walking stick to aid her, Ella set off.

"Aren't we going to see Hansel and Gretel?" Tomcat voiced as Ella backtracked the way they had come, circled around the square, avoiding the water fountain, and headed towards Willow stationed outside the Gatehouse Inn.

Ella nodded. "First, I want a word with Willow."

"What do you think will happen to Mr Puddles?" Tomcat looked up with big wide green eyes.

Ella looked away as if concentrating on navigating the cobblestones. "I hate to think... But if Mr Puddles is dangerous, I guess they will do what they must." Tomcat's ears dipped and Ella shared his low mood. While she grieved for Arthur, she struggled to believe Mr Puddles could really have been responsible for her friend's death. There was something strange going on here, and she was going to find out the truth.

Was it possible another vicious dog had done the deed and Mr Puddles was merely a scapedog? No, that didn't seem likely. How could there be another dog attacking townsfolk with no one being the wiser? There would have been big paw prints or something left behind.

As Ella approached the younger woman, she observed that Willow was giving away the baked goods in her basket, not selling them as she assumed. That was clever. People could seldom resist a free sample. "Do you have any date scones, my dear?" Ella asked. "I'm partial to a date scone."

"Brownie," whispered Tomcat from the crook of her arm.

"Or a brownie," Ella added, resisting the urge to look down at the cat in her arms.

"Good mother Ella, I'm so glad to see you." Willow set her basket down, her bracelets and amulets jingling as she did so, and she gestured to the empty basket. "I'm afraid I just gave away the last brownie. But if you come by my bakery over on Fifth Street this evening, I'll gladly have an entire fresh tray for you. The twins told me you might be able to help with Mr Puddles. It's absurd what that guardswoman is saying he did."

"I don't recall any bakeries on Fifth," Ella murmured, casting through her memory of the eclectic bunch of antique shops and book shops tucked along the narrow street.

"It used to be a tea shop."

"Oh dear," Ella voiced before she could stop herself. "You don't mean Ginger Brewed?"

"That's the one! Although it seems I will have to rename it. Nearly everyone I have given directions to today has reacted in the same way as you!" She placed her hands on her hips. "Maybe you would do me the kindness of telling me why everyone baulks?"

Ella chewed her bottom lip. No one enjoyed hearing bad news, but it was kinder than keeping the truth from her. "Many years ago, Charmington was ravaged by a magical fever. People called it the black fever because one of the first signs of infection was that fingertips turned black. I'm afraid the first victims worked at Ginger's."

"And so what, people still think there's danger?" Willow retorted, flabbergasted. "That's just what I need on top of everything else."

Ella nodded in sympathy. "People have long memories. A lot of young women died."

"I'm starting to think I'm cursed." Willow rifled through the many amulets and charms strung about her neck. At last, she appeared to find the one she wanted, a chunky rose quartz crystal, and she pressed it to her forehead, closed her eyes, and hummed.

Ella watched her for a moment. "What were you saying about the twins?"

Willow stopped humming and opened one eye. "Millie, or maybe Sally, said you have influence with the queen. Please, help me get my poodle back. I know he didn't hurt that man, I know it."

Ella exchanged a look with Tomcat. "Arthur was my very good friend, and I want to find out what happened to him. I promise you I'll go talk to Cassidy on your behalf."

Tomcat nodded.

Ella caught Willow's eye. "Last night, you said, in Nottingham, were-infected rats killed your neighbour's cat. I don't want to cause offence, but is it possible they passed the infection on to Mr Puddles? Is that how he lost his ear?"

Willow paled. "I didn't think of that!" She ran her hands through her already mussed-up orange hair. "No, it can't be true. He's not infected. I'm sure."

"Enough debate!" rang out from across the square as Van Helsing shouted to the crowd. "Fetch the Baker! Stake him out, and tonight's full moon will reveal the truth!"

Oh dear, were the townsfolk actually considering Baker Bron might be a werewolf? How ridiculous.

CHAPTER II

NOT WATT'S SON

221 BAKER STREET, CHARMINGTON.

Ella patted Willow's hand. "Head home, my dear. I'll go talk to Cassidy."

"Thank you! I'm sure you understand what Mr Puddles means to me." Willow took off one of her amulets and looped it over Tomcat's head. "A charm of good fortune for your own precious pet."

Ella pinched up the small round pendant between her fingers for closer examination. A silver charm. Protection against werewolves. Hmm...

Willow scooped up her empty basket when, suddenly, the three little orphan boys wearing matching blue and yellow striped sweaters, who had been playing boats at the fountain, flocked around her and begged for treats. She placated them with a few wrapped sweets from her pockets and invited them to follow her home, as she had to refill the goodies basket anyway. Waving farewell to Ella, the children trailed after Willow, but then the smallest boy doubled back and pressed something into Ella's hand, saying, "Clever cat, missus."

The boy ran off to catch up with the others, and Ella regarded the item now in her palm. A crumpled piece of newspaper.

Tomcat peered in as she unfolded the scrap. "What's it say?"

It was a corner ripped from the *Nottingham Times*. Handwritten on one side was an address: 221 Baker Street. C.

"Baker Street? What's on Baker Street?"

NEITHER BAKERS NOR BAKERIES WERE situated on Baker Street. It was a quiet working-class residential area. A row of packed-in terrace houses, the ground floors were stone, the top two levels of wood and plaster jutted out over the narrow street. Most of the houses were split into pairs A and B.

Ella scanned the numbers adorning the well-kept doors. 221 was a double-width house. Its neighbours were 119 A and B, and 223 A and B.

Hmm. She eyed the window grates set at street level. All the houses along this terrace had basements. Perhaps the basements had been divided into further accommodation? Charmington was built on a thermal seam and warm basements would have a lot of appeal now winter reigned.

She peered over a wrought-iron staircase railing that led down to the basement at 221. A cloaked figure stood on the bottom step.

The hooded figure pushed their cowl back. Cassidy Turpin. "I was starting to wonder if the Baker Street boys hadn't found you," the guardswoman said, beckoning Ella down the metal steps to the basement door.

"I wasn't sure if this was the address..." Ella regarded the door set below street level. At first glance, it was unremarkable, but closer inspection revealed the wood was reinforced with steel rivets, and a sliding panel was inset high to act as a peephole. An oddly sturdy door for a respectable residential street. "There is no 221 C."

Cassidy cocked an eyebrow, apparently confused. Then shook her head and laughed. "Not 221 *C*. C for Cassidy."

"Oh," Ella replied flatly, to curb her embarrassment. She patted Tomcat absentmindedly. He looked up at her and shrugged, as if to say *Easy mistake to make.*

Cassidy fixed Ella with a stern gaze. "What I'm about to show you, I must have your solemn promise will remain between us." But then rather lessened the gravity by yawning.

Ella regarded the young guardswoman critically. The poor woman was clearly bone-tired. "Shouldn't you be in bed if you're night watch? When was the last time you had a proper night's sleep?"

Cassidy flashed a grin. "Funny you say that. I have you to thank for my lack of sleep. I've been having to cover extra day shifts due to Axel's time in the lockup."

"Oh, well," Ella found herself abashed, unsure where Cassidy's loyalties lay, but her concern was proven unfounded when Cassidy patted her on the shoulder and added,

"And thanks to those extra day shifts, I've finally made progress on uncovering a smuggling ring that Axel has been turning a blind eye to for years!" After unlocking the stout door, she led them down a short corridor into a double-height, well-lit work-room that was filled with all-manner of half-finished contraptions, mostly models. Models of ships, carriages, kites and airships. And in the centre of the room, several tables had been pushed together and were covered by a detailed scale model of their walled township.

"Magic preserve," Ella whispered, setting Tomcat on the tabletop, and they both studied the model of Charmington. There was the castle, the town walls featuring every gatehouse, the various town squares, prominent buildings, and even tiny strings of street lights. "Did you make this?"

"Not me. Ace, my MT guy."

"Em tee?" Sometimes it was like the youth spoke another language.

"Magic tech," Cassidy explained with no hint of condescension.

"Oh," Ella intoned, struck by comprehension, "you mean a *craftsman*."

Cassidy scythed a hand under her chin. "Don't let Ace hear you calling him a craftsman."

"Craftsman," hissed a voice from under the table. "My father—my grandfather—was a craftsman! I'm a magical technician."

There was a *click,* and the street lights on the model town suddenly lit up. A second later, a small fellow, about three feet high, dressed in a leather apron over work clothes, popped out from under the tables and peered up at Ella through rose-coloured spectacles balanced on the end of a long, thin nose. He held out a tiny hand to her and said, "Heard what you did for Rum."

Ella shook the tiny hand warmly. "I'm only sorry I couldn't have done more."

A month ago, Rum, a craftsman and the owner of the Crossroads tavern located deep in Wyld Enchantment Woods, had been killed—*murdered*—by Axel, the head of Queen Sibylla's henchmen—or captain of the guards to give him his official title. Yet no one had seen the incident. It was Ella's word against Axel's. Sibylla had only given Axel sixty days in the town lockup—half of which had now been served.

Ace shrugged. "You spoke out. My people know." He narrowed his dark, intelligent eyes. "Just like they know who turns a blind eye."

Ella bit her lip. He meant her sister Sibylla. Something about Ace's countenance and mannerisms nudged a memory. Could it be Ace was related to Watt, the former craftsman to the royal court, who Sibylla had stripped of his position when she came to power?

"Are you Watt's son?"

Ace shook his head while climbing a stepladder up the side of the table. "I'm not Watt's son. He was my grandfather." Ace reached over a section of replica wall to adjust something in the model when Tomcat peeped up from the Northgate Square where he'd been crouched. Ace lurched back, did a double-take, flicked up the rose-coloured lens and then popped them down over his eyes again. "Epp!" Ace turned and jumped off the table.

Tomcat sat in the middle of the scale model, his fluffy tail flicking across the model unicorn fountain where he'd been playing with soap boats in real life earlier that day. "What did I do?"

Cassidy raised a finger. "That cat can talk..."

"About that," Ella began while Ace yanked a cardboard box stacked off to the side and tipped the contents out, spilling strings of fairy lights across the floorboards.

"Here, kitty, kitty," Ace coaxed, dragging the box next to the table. "What a lovely empty box!"

"Ooh!" Tomcat stretched his neck up and swayed like a snake as if the sight was irresistible. "I love boxes!" He sprang off the table into the awaiting box.

"Aha!" Ace cried, slamming down the flaps and signalling Cassidy to help him.

"Why are we trapping Miss Ella's cat?" Cassidy asked, holding the lid closed as Ace removed his spectacles and held them out for the young guardswoman. She put them on and then lifted up one flap and peered cautiously inside.

"It's dark in here!" complained Tomcat.

"You don't see that every day..." Cassidy whistled. "What exactly am I looking at?"

"It's a hostile corporeal entity!" Ace exclaimed gleefully, but then he frowned as if a dark thought had occurred. "A spy, perhaps, for you know who?"

"Dumb it down for me. What're you saying?" Cassidy replied, removing the spectacles. "You should see this." She handed the spectacles to Ella.

Ella uncrossed her arms and slipped the rose-coloured spectacles on. Inside the box, a swirling purple light glowed from within Tomcat. Several strands trailed off his body and snaked from the room, back the way they'd come, like a cord or a leash.

"It's not just a cat," Ace explained to Cassidy. "Its body is hosting another being. Like a magical parasite."

Ella removed the glasses and returned them to Ace. "I know."

"You know?!" Cassidy blurted.

"Can I see?" Tomcat enquired hopefully, pushing his little cat face up through the flaps as Cassidy endeavoured to smoosh him back down.

"It's all right, my dear. You can let him out," Ella said. And then she told the pair how Tom April, the newest henchman to join Sibylla's employment at the castle, had blundered into her garden and accidentally swapped bodies with her cat Tilly due to an ill-timed wish and a shooting star, and now Tom's injured human body lay encased in a giant pumpkin in a kind of magical stasis.

Cassidy and Ace exchanged glances and then released their hold on the box. Tomcat leapt out. "Please, can I see too?"

"Uh," Cassidy replied, looking around helplessly. "Ace, do you have a mirror?"

Ace nodded and disappeared to return a minute later with a small hand mirror that might be part of a dressing-table set. Cassidy held the mirror while Ace placed the glasses over Tomcat's feline nose.

"Wow! Is that my essence? It's so pretty!" Tomcat's whiskers fanned in delight. He waved a paw and then lifted each foot in turn. "What are all those trails of light?"

Ace gently removed the spectacles and slipped them into the front pocket of his leather apron. "Think of a kite. The strings anchor your consciousness, what you called your essence, all the way back to your real body."

"Wow! That's so neat!"

"Indeed. But you need to protect that pumpkin..." The little man's expression turned grim as he looked up at Ella. "If the strings get cut, the essence won't be able to find its way back. He'll be stuck as a cat forever."

CHAPTER 12

RED FLAGS

"Forever?" repeated Tomcat.

Ace nodded, but then amended, "Or, at least, until the hosting cat's body dies."

Ella clicked her tongue thoughtfully. That made sense. "Tom, this is why I've been telling you to be cautious. Axel bears us both a grudge. What would he do if he found out you're still alive and vulnerable?"

"I know you're right, but I thought he was my friend." Tomcat sighed.

"So, that's what happened to Tom April," Cassidy murmured, still sitting on the floor. "I was starting to believe the rumours that you'd run off to Nottingham with Ginny Bron."

Tomcat bunted his head against her knee. "Did you miss me? I wanted to come and tell you, but I didn't want to get you in trouble."

"This is so weird." She stood up and dusted her trousers. "I'm talking to a cat."

"I'm still the same Tom April," Tomcat insisted, his little ears dipping.

"Of course." She looked away. "It's just going to take some time getting used to."

Ella frowned. Poor Tom. She coughed to break the tension. "Earlier, I was under the assumption you wanted to speak with me? I had hoped you had insight into Arthur's tragic death. Do you think someone other than Mr Puddles is to blame?"

Cassidy appeared to give herself a mental shake. "Maybe. Just bear with me, this is a long story."

"If that's the case," Ella interrupted, "is there a chair I can sit in?" She lifted her walking stick to emphasise her point. Ace immediately wheeled over a chair from one of the desks, and Ella nodded her thanks as she settled down. "Your grandfather made this for me," Ella told him, meaning her stick. "When I first lost my wand, I could barely walk. The pain of all my years unleashed was excruciating."

"May I have a closer look?" Ace asked politely, little hands already held out.

"By all means," Ella replied, bemused, handing the stick over. He skipped over to a desk and held it under a magnifying glass. She turned back to Cassidy. "Please go on, my dear."

Cassidy gestured to the town model, all business once more. "For years now, there's been established smuggling points along the town wall. Each red flag represents places where drop boxes have been discovered more than once. Always during the full moon."

Ella sat up straighter to better survey the little flags marking the wall. There were seven flags in total. Four were red. The other three were black, and numbered one through three. The third one marked Arthur's wall-side property just inside the northern gates. "Drop boxes?"

Cassidy scooped up the fairy lights Ace had tipped out back into the box. "Like this one. Boxes that are lowered over the inside of the wall via a rope and pulley, or just thrown if the contents can withstand the drop."

"And what are they filled with? Not fairy lights, surely?"

"Actually, yes, for the most part. Low-level magical items, like the lights, sure-fire charms to keep fires burning overnight, memory portraits, that kind of thing. Little domestic items that make life more comfortable. Although technically they're banned, the watch has turned a blind eye because they've always been harmless."

"What's changed?" Tomcat asked, leaping up on the table.

"About a year ago, a drop box was reported here." Cassidy tapped the black flag numbered one, located on the southern part of the wall, very close to the south gate.

Ella hummed to herself. Southgate was where Hansel and Gretel lived. Their coaching stables and the Huntsman tavern were the first buildings inside the gate.

"It fell into the garden of an elderly couple, here. The elderly gentleman resident interrupted the receiver—who we suspect had been waiting in the garden of the house next door, which had been vacant for a few months."

Ella narrowed her eyes. The Cheltons and Bron the baker also lived in that neighbourhood. "The smugglers on the outside of the wall got their positioning a little off that time?"

"Yes. Now, when that's happened before, the interceptor on the inside leaves the package rather than risk being caught themselves. However, this time, rather than leave the box, they bludgeoned the husband. Fortunately, one of the neighbours—"

"Hansel?" Ella interrupted a guess.

"No, you would think so, but he was out of town. Chelton the butcher scared off the receiver but kept his package."

"What was in the box?" Tomcat's hackles rose.

"Buried within a bundle of fairy lights was a vial of green ink."

Ella folded her arms and raised an eyebrow. She waited for Cassidy to continue.

"A few nights later, someone accidentally set fire to Hansel's business. We think they must have been trying to recover the package from the Chelton's next door. Only instead, they started a fire in a mad dash to escape Gretel's clutches. Clearly, they had no idea what Hansel and Gretel *are*. Gretel surprised them, and they quote, 'Drop candle on curtains and scream like baby.'"

Ella and Tomcat exchanged glances. They had been at the Huntsman tavern a month before and seen the fire damage to the top floor of the building. "Did she catch him?"

Cassidy sucked air between her teeth. "Unfortunately, no. According to Gretel, she was laughing so hard by the time she finished counting—er, she likes to count to fifty, to um, give people a chance to outrun her..."

Ella's lips pushed out in a facial shrug. "Indeed? Well, anyone who knows Gretel knows her sense of humour is a little dark."

"Anyway," Cassidy continued, "Gretel realised she had to put out the fire, and so the intruder got away. But she confirmed it was the same person that Chelton scared off."

"Chelton doesn't talk. Did he write down what the thug looked like?" Ella leaned back on the chair. My, it was comfy. The armrests were carved just right, and the base was on springs. Ace definitely knew his craft. She glanced over at him and was startled to see her walking stick broken down into various parts, exposing the stiletto blade in the centre, which she'd all but forgotten was hidden inside.

"No, but he did a remarkable little watercolour portrait," Cassidy explained. "Wasn't it good, Ace?"

"Quite remarkable," Ace murmured as if not really listening. He had a polishing cloth in one hand and was applying oil into one of the chambers on her walking stick.

"I've always wanted to learn watercolours," Tomcat added wistfully, placing a paw under his chin, elbow resting on the model town wall. "Did you recognise the person?"

Cassidy nodded and, after rifling in a map cabinet, the surface of which was strewn with odd little models of what appeared to be carriages but had no place to hitch the horse, she handed Ella a printed wanted poster, with an engraved line drawing of a thin-faced man, who apparently went by the alias Rooster. "He was a notorious Nottingham pickpocket in his youth. Now escalated to less subtle and more violent crimes, bag snatching, housebreaking, often stabbing or slashing victims' throats to silence them."

"Oh dear," murmured Ella, imagining the horror faced by the old couple whose lives he'd threatened. "Thank goodness Chelton was there."

Cassidy took the poster and placed it on the table for Tom to see.

"What was so special about the ink?" Ella asked.

"At first, we were baffled, but Ace here—" She nodded to her MT guy, who puffed his little chest slightly while putting the walking stick back together again. "—ran tests, and concluded it was Pendragon green."

"It's what they use to print their paper banknotes in Avalon," Ace explained before Ella could ask. "It's a restricted item, manufactured onsite at the Camelot mint. It's prohibited from being shipped outside of the country."

"I don't understand," Ella voiced, rocking back on the springy desk chair. "We don't use Avalon currency, so if someone were to forge their banknotes here, you couldn't spend them. You'd have to go all the way to Nottingham to exchange them. And even assuming someone went to that much trouble, surely a vial wouldn't print more than a few banknotes?"

Ace nodded, running the polishing cloth over the reassembled walking stick. "Agreed. But last month, a drop box was found at flag two. Again a vial of printer's ink was hidden within fairy lights."

The moon had been full last night. "And last night, flag three," Ella guessed, her stomach clenched and she felt dizzy. "The third drop box was found at Arthur's."

Cassidy and Ace nodded.

"And the Rooster fellow?" she leaned forward. "You think he killed Arthur over the box?"

CHAPTER 13

QUESTIONING EXPECTATIONS

"There's been no sightings of Rooster within Charmington since he escaped Gretel." Cassidy shook her head. "Last we heard, he'd been incarcerated in Nottingham prison, eight months ago. And besides that, the drop box wasn't taken. We found it this morning."

"Oh, of course," murmured Ella, "otherwise you wouldn't even know about it... And so, what do you require from me?" she voiced, sitting further forward. "While I appreciate your candour, I can't imagine you fill in every Charmington resident on official watch business."

Cassidy and Ace exchanged glances, and it struck Ella there was something they weren't telling her. Perhaps they wanted her to run some banned magical tests and give Ace a hand? It had been some time since she'd done anything of the sort.

"There was a breakout recently from the Nottingham prison," Ace explained. "But Rooster's name wasn't on the list of escapees."

"Oh dear," Ella tutted. "Well, I guess it's good to be able to rule him out."

"That's the thing. According to rumours, Prince John and his cronies have grossly understated the number of prisoners who broke out."

Ella sat back as the penny dropped, and her enthusiasm turned to hollow disappointment. They didn't ask her here to help. Not really. "And you're hoping I can use my connections to get an official list of escapees?"

Cassidy stepped forward. "We don't need a full list. We just want to be able to rule out Rooster, or not, as the case may be."

Ella looked down at her hands. Foolish old woman, she scolded herself. Why else would they need you? Is that your pride poking you in the chest? Well, swallow it down and remember you're here for your friend Arthur. If the only use you can be is buttering up Sibylla and that odd Prince John to get some list that will help the real doers solve what happened to Arthur, then that's what you'll do.

"I'm at your service. And now, I must be going. I have a busy day ahead," Ella fibbed, pushing herself to her feet. "My stick, please, Ace, and may I keep that poster of Rooster?"

Cassidy handed the wanted poster over and pointed to the ear of Rooster's engraved portrait. "According to what Gretel said, the left side of his face or ear was burnt when his hair caught fire. It may have scarred."

"Understood. Look for a person with facial burns." Ella neatly folded the wanted poster away, tucking it safely into her cloak pocket along with Tom's letter.

"Before we go, I have a question," Tomcat said, raising a paw like he was in school. "Why would the smugglers change their routine from an out-of-the-way, empty building to a prominent, occupied one? That's such a risk."

"A very good point," Ella said. "It seems a poor choice. Could it have been an accident?"

"We think they were expecting Arthur to be away," Cassidy added. "As you noted, a few vials here and there isn't going to sustain a full-scale forgery operation. We've been theorising for some time they will increase the volume of ink. And a few months back, Hansel commented that he, the Cheltons and the baker, had been receiving a lot of unsolicited mail. Competitions to win holidays in exotic destinations. That kind of thing. I borrowed some of the pamphlets he'd been sent and showed them to all the businesses located within one hundred metres of every gatehouse, including Arthur's. They had all received them.

"Further digging revealed Arthur had been approached several times by strangers enquiring if his business was for sale—twice in the last month alone. Ace and I theorised the forgers plan to take over a business located close to a gatehouse. Say a tavern or similar, one that often receives deliveries. Ink in wine bottles would make a good disguise."

"No one would look twice." Ella nodded slowly. "A busy place like that, the bustle itself would provide a certain cover..."

She thought over what Willow had been saying last night about her business not being what she expected and complaining about Arthur's business. And she was a newcomer! Could it be she had been sent from Nottingham by this forgery outfit—whether she knew it or not? A willing or unwitting dupe to help maintain cover for the smugglers or whoever?

And she owned Mr Puddles! Could it be possible she had *trained* the dog to kill? Mr Puddles was certainly behaving aggressively when he arrived at the haberdashery... Was there time for her to set Mr

Puddles on Arthur *before* arriving at Book Club? All she had to do then was *not* tie Mr Puddles up properly and the alibi created itself!

Ace returned the walking stick, saying, "I've fixed the light." He demonstrated, tapping the end of the walking stick twice against the ground in quick succession. A bright light flooded out from near the base, illuminating a pool of light six feet across.

"Thank you," Ella replied, clasping the stick and tapping the tip twice against the floor again to turn the light off. "That feature hasn't worked properly for years. Much appreciated."

Tomcat jumped down from the table as Cassidy gave them one last caution. "If you happen to see Rooster, do not approach him. You can always get word to me via one of the Baker Street boys. If you need to hold him, get one of the other guards if you have to, but don't endanger yourself. Promise me."

Ella nodded, not meeting the guardswoman's eye. "Lawks, wouldn't dream of anything else. Apprehending Rooster myself is the furthest thing from my mind. Trust me." She smiled in what she hoped was a convincing fashion. "And what is to happen to Mr Puddles? I presume from your line of inquiry that you have ruled the dog out."

Cassidy pulled a face. "Officially, the watch stance is Arthur was killed by the dog. If we keep openly investigating this case. we'll scare off the smugglers."

"But you won't let anything happen to him? Can I assume Mr Puddles will be returned safely to his owner in due course?"

Cassidy and Ace shared a look.

Eventually, Cassidy said, "In due course."

Hmm... Ella thought. They were definitely keeping something from her. But what? And why?

CHAPTER 14

DIABOLICAL PLOTS

STREETS OF CHARMINGTON.

"Ella, what are you plotting?" Tomcat asked, his tone low and suspicious while trotting nimbly at her side as she marched down Baker Street, her walking stick tapping a determined beat on the cobbles.

"Lawks, why assume I'm thinking anything other than my typical old-lady concerns?" she replied, her pace increasing, only slowing to return a polite nod to people who doffed their caps or bobbed a curtsey as she passed.

"Because you always walk fast when you're plotting something *and* you've got your sneaky face on," Tomcat stated. "Plus, I couldn't help but notice that we're heading *away* from the castle—which is where I assumed we'd go first if you actually planned on asking Sibylla to get that list of escaped prisoners."

"Sneaky face?" Ella paused to glance into a corner shop window and observe her reflection. "Magic preserve me, you are right." She suppressed her smile and frowned instead. "Is this better? Do I look like I'm contemplating my supper and the lack of respect young people show to their elders?"

Tomcat sat at the foot of a gaslamp. "Whatever you're up to, I should be included—Arthur was my friend too!' He waved a paw back in the general direction of Baker Street. "And besides, did you see? I'm a guardsman, and yet Cassidy treated me, like, like a cat!"

Ella let out a long breath. Ahh, here was the crunch. "Take it from me, you can't force people to like you."

"What?" Tomcat blustered, forgetting his cat act and standing up on his hind legs. "I don't *like* her—I respect her as a fellow guard. Sure, she's got a nice smile and she smells like apricot blossoms, but, but..." He looked down and toed a cobblestone. "Maybe I like her. A little."

"Give her time. If it's meant to be, it will," Ella soothed, trying to offer some perspective. "After all, it would be odd if she fancies you while you are still a cat."

"Yeah, I guess." Tomcat shrugged half-heartedly. "I just don't feel like a cat. Y'know?"

Of course, she did. Better than anyone. She was also dismissed as either an old lady or used as some political asset by which to gain influence. Why couldn't they just see her as Ella? The only person who had ever treated her as an equal was Richard.

"Think of this time as an opportunity. Cassidy gets to meet your mind, not your strong yet gentle arms." Ella waved off the peculiar look he gave her. "Ignore me, I was repeating something I saw Tobias had written. But that reminds me, what of young Miss Harper? There's a young lady already enamoured of your charms. Perhaps when you're returned to your body, you could court her?"

Tomcat looked confused. "I don't know any...oh, wait, the girl at the post office. No, I don't, I mean, she seemed real nice and stuff but..."

Ella only nodded. The heart wanted what the heart wanted. Well, that was probably for the best. Imagine having Harold Harper for an in-law!

"Come along," she said, "we'll plot while we walk."

"So, you think Rooster is to blame?"

"I'd be foolish to rule it out," Ella replied, pausing for a cart to roll by before they crossed the road. "But while I'm no expert on the minds of smugglers and thieves, if I was them, I wouldn't involve Rooster again after that horrendous failure to collect a simple box. Unless he was the mastermind of the whole endeavour—and someone who panics as he did doesn't sound like mastermind material to me. No, these people want to go unnoticed. If they want to move their items freely in and out of the town, then they themselves need to be able to move freely—wanted criminals can hardly do that—so they will appear ordinary. But first things first. Do you recall what time we left Arthur's?"

"Ahh, well, I heard the clock tower strike eight just after we arrived at the haberdashery, so at a guess maybe seven fifty?"

"It was exactly a quarter to eight. I remember looking at the clock tower. Now, do you recall Arthur was found just before nine thirty?"

"Yes! Cassidy was pretending to write a citation! She mentioned the time."

"Precisely. Now my question is, were you and I the last people to speak to Arthur or was there someone else?"

"What? Who? Do you suspect someone?"

"Maybe it escaped your notice, but when we came upon Hansel and Gretel they were discussing Arthur."

"Oh! Yes! And Gretel said something about warning Hansel not to go and talk to him! Do you think he did? Do you think that's where Hansel went? Wait, you don't think Hansel had anything to do with Arthur's death, do you?"

"Certainly not. But Hansel arrived to collect Gretel, I think, a bit before nine. If Hansel was the last person to speak to Arthur, then that helps us narrow the timeframe down to around that half hour before he was found. It also means Arthur wasn't killed straight after we left."

"Why is that important?"

"Because that rules Willow out."

"Wait! What?" bellowed Tomcat and Ella was grateful that over the noise of a passing cart and horse hooves on cobbles, his voice wasn't very audible. "You can't think she did it! When? Between us leaving at seven forty-five and her arriving at Book Club, which couldn't have been more than five past eight!"

"That's still at least a quarter of an hour—even if she only had ten minutes, that's still plenty of time to do the deed and then get to Book Club at just after eight. It all hangs on what Hansel has to say, doesn't it? If he went and spoke to Arthur straight after we left him, then Willow couldn't have had the time."

"I just can't see why you suspect her! Aside from the fact she's lovely, she could hardly be an assassin or something because she clangs like a church bell with every step! I never saw someone with so much jewellery. It would take at least five minutes to take off those bracelets and put them back on! And are you actually saying she's framing her own poodle? No one is so diabolical."

CHAPTER 15

THE BAKER AND THE HUNTSMAN

BRON'S BAKERY, SOUTHGATE SQUARE, CHARMINGTON.

Southgate Square was busier than Ella had seen for years. A dozen citizens, most of whom she recognised from the unicorn fountain gathering that morning, were hovering quite close, but not too close, to the bakery. There was no sign of their ringleader, that odorous Van Helsing man.

Typical. Loud-mouthed, irresponsible people were always quick in inciting others to action and yet somehow never around when things turned sour.

Baker Bron was on the steps of his business, his neighbours Chelton the butcher and wife Martha by his side. Together facing off against a barrage of questions and accusations from irate townsfolk.

"I am not a werewolf!" Bron shouted, pleading, looking to Martha and Chelton for support.

"Aye, so he ain't," Martha replied, between sucking on her clay pipe and jetting little puffs of caramel-scented smoke into the frosty air. "If Bron be a werewolf, sure as eggs are eggs, my love would know." Chelton the butcher, a very large man with a gruff and hairy exterior but gentle and quiet intention, nodded.

"All we're saying is, *prove* it," one of the gathered masses replied— Tobias the school teacher, Ella realised with dismay. "Let us chain you up under the full moon tonight."

"Chain me? This is madness!" Bron clutched at his temples, fingers digging into his hair, when he caught sight of Ella. "Good mother Ella, you can vouch for me!"

The crowd parted to let her through. "What is all this fuss about?"

"Be careful, Lady Ella, don't stand too close," someone cautioned from the throng. "He might bite—their bite is mighty infectious. Everyone knows a newly turned werewolf can't control themselves."

"I'm not a werewolf," Bron wailed. "I was bitten by a regular wolf, not a werebeast! Good mother Ella, you remember seeing me last month—wasn't I out under the full moon then?"

The last time Ella had seen Bron out in Wyld Enchantment Woods was when he was standing over the human body of Tom April, who had been shot by an arrow and left for dead. Ella had made Bron drag Tom's body to her cottage so she might try to save his life. Certainly, Bron hadn't been a werewolf, but he also hadn't been a very charitable neighbour, and Ella had to bully him into doing the right thing due to the baker's hatred of the guards, thanks to Axel having an affair with his wife. "Hmm. That little I can vouch for."

"See? See?" Bron implored the people, who had come in a bit closer and were all trying to shield themselves behind Ella while appearing resolute in their purpose at the same time.

"Maybe the infection hadn't taken hold then," Tobias argued, holding up a rather large book that Ella beheld with a sense of dread, guessing it was probably *The Guide to Creatures of Wyld Kingdom* her brother Merlin had penned. "Says right here..." He thumbed through a few pages and read aloud, "In some rare cases the infection can lay dormant for years, only triggered by extreme physical or mental stress."

"This is a matter of public safety!" another woman piped up, a dribbling baby tucked under one arm and holding a thick length of chain in the other. "I have my little orphans to think of!"

And yet she brought her babe within arms' reach of a suspected werewolf?

The woman hefted the steel chain. "I insist you chain yourself up in a public square so decent people can cut your head off when you turn into a rabid beast!"

"Decent?" Ella folded her arms. Clearly, decency was measured on a very long and twisty sliding scale by some. She glanced over to the neighbouring buildings, her attention drawn to the fire damage on the top floor at the Huntsman tavern. Did she see something move between the gaps of the boarded-over upstairs window where a board was missing? Yes... Someone was watching them. "Everyone, calm down," she insisted, tapping her cane twice and inadvertently turning the light on.

As one, the masses stepped back with suspicious murmurs of *magic!*

"We are decent folk. We don't hold with the likes of magic here!" the woman with the baby and chain retorted, pointing an accusing finger at the pool of light.

"'T ain't magic, Mistress Fairweather," Martha mocked, "you dim-witted fishwife. Anyone can see that walking stick be simple craftsman mechanicals."

"Fishwife, am I?" Mistress Fairweather snapped, turning her ire on the butcher's wife. "That's rich coming from the likes of you, Martha Chelton. You grew up on Hot Cockle Lane!"

"Ladies, ladies," Tobias tried to intercede. "Let's not resort to name-calling—we have a werewolf to deal with."

"Suspected werewolf!" Bron wailed.

"Aha! So, he admits it!"

Ella ducked out of the crowd as the tide was turning darker against Bron and made her escape across to the Huntsman tavern. where Tomcat was sitting on the porch, his white tail flicking. "Not going well?"

Ella tapped the cane against the steps to quell the light. "Never try and reason with a mob," she muttered under her breath. When would she learn? "I think they're going to be here a while yet. You keep an eye on them and come tell me if things get messy. I'll go talk to Hansel."

"See if they have any bar snacks. I'm hungry."

ELLA ENTERED THE WINDOWLESS TAVERN'S common room. Dusty chairs were stacked up on tables. Walls lined with shelves housed yellowing skulls and bottles filled with ancient and mysterious substances. She stood blinking in the half-light, waiting for her eyes to adjust to the gloom, contemplating reigniting the walking stick luminance, when a deep, smooth voice from the shadows intoned, "Lady Ella, we meet again."

A man dressed in black leather, knives belted at either hip, exuding a presence both frightening and yet somehow alluring, was seated at the bar. Prince John's bodyguard—or, as Ella suspected from their previous encounter—Prince John's house assassin or some other 'fixer' of a dubious nature.

He turned his head, revealing a handsome face about thirty years old, dark hair streaked with a stripe of white at his right temple, and his eyes. My, what big eyes he had. Dark smouldering eyes. Eyes that drank in her presence, like he could suck her soul straight out of her body... What was his name? They hadn't been properly introduced last time.

He raised a glass of bright red liquid. "Join me for a cranberry? My treat."

Ella swallowed down her apprehension. Magic preserve, he could probably hear her heart beating. "Thank you, that's very kind, Mr...er?"

Prince John's bodyguard's brow creased, like a statue winking, a tiny crack of surprise from a man used to making an indelible impression. "You don't remember me?"

Ella chose a barstool beside him and levered herself up on it. "Of course, I do, you were with John at the archery contest last month. But official introductions weren't made." She removed her glove and extended her hand. "Ella Charming, at your service."

The bodyguard regarded the offered hand, and then, quite seriously, took her hand in his, leaned forward and slowly kissed the back of her bare fingers.

If Ella had been in the habit of gossiping with her girlfriends, then the retelling of this encounter would have started with 'Yowie!' As it was, she wasn't in the habit and instead found herself holding her breath as his lips left a warmth on her skin, a light touch like smoke.

"As I am at yours, my lady."

Across his own bare knuckles, Ella observed the scar she had noticed last month, a half-moon pattern, like a bite... He withdrew his touch and placed an elbow on the bar top, the movement drawing attention to the chunky silver manacle he wore overtop of his fitted leather sleeve. Odd for a man in his line of business to wear such a prominent piece of jewellery.

Grinning, he sat back, a hand to his face as if to hide a smile. What was he laughing at? As if undecided himself, he shrugged. A languid motion, somehow both casual and yet threatening at the same time. Yet, there was nothing casual about this mysterious man, he was clearly quite deliberate. "John calls me Wulf. That will do for our purposes."

CHAPTER 16

DANGEROUS OR DREAMY?

HUNTSMAN TAVERN, SOUTHGATE SQUARE, CHARMINGTON.

"Cranberry?" Wulf picked up an earthenware jug from the counter and poured them a glass each. She took the offered cranberry and copied him in raising the cool vessel in salute. "To our betters and the chains that bind us."

Ella swallowed down the tart liquid. The freshness and crisp taste snapped her senses, and she found whatever spell he'd cast on her was broken. Blinking, she looked around the otherwise empty room. She was here on a purpose and had pressing business—she had no time to ogle a charming newcomer. "Is Hansel out the back?"

Wulf shook his head, stood up, and leaned over the bar to extract a bottle of whiskey tucked out of sight under the counter. "Off to Nottingham, last night." Sitting back down, he uncapped the whiskey and arched an eyebrow in a gesture of enquiry.

"None for me, thank you." Ella balled a fist, cursing her forgetfulness. Of course, the full moon meant the brother and sister were off on their monthly stagecoach run to Nottingham, and wouldn't be back until the middle of the week at the earliest, depending on the state of the roads.

As Wulf poured himself a tumbler, Ella placed her glass beside his. "Changed my mind..." She waited while he poured the amber liquid, annoyed at herself for forgetting the stagecoach schedule. That's probably where they headed straight after Hansel collected Gretel from Book Club. She sighed. Her plan to question Hansel was foiled.

"What brings you here, Wulf? Is Prince John in Charmington?" If he was, no doubt Sibylla would expect Ella to entertain him rather than deal with the prince herself.

"You catch me in rather an awkward position," Wulf started, which Ella found highly doubtful. Wulf was clearly the type to do all the catching. She pushed the random thought away as he continued, "I'm here unofficially. A prisoner of ours has escaped over our border into yours. I'd appreciate it if you didn't inform Her Majesty. No need to alarm anyone." He scooped up one of Ella's hands and held it gently, regarding her with his deep, dark eyes. "Can I entrust you to keep my secret?"

Yowie.

Ella untangled her fingers as the front door creaked open and Tomcat squeezed in. She patted her cloak and withdrew the wanted poster from the pocket. "Is this who you're chasing, Mr Wulf?"

Wulf sat up, all business once more, and smoothed the poster flat with a smile. "Ahh, Rooster, that rascal, though looking less pretty last I saw him, what with having an ear burned off." He slid the poster back over to her. "Rooster is secured within our prison system and won't be released until next month."

"Are you sure? There was a terrible murder last night."

"You have my word," Wulf said as Tomcat leapt up onto the counter and navigated between the glasses. "Out of professional interest, who was killed?"

"Arthur, at the Gatehouse Inn. I was hoping Hansel could—"

"The Gatehouse?" Wulf interrupted, standing up and pushing the chair back when, suddenly, Tomcat pinned Wulf's right hand to the bar top with his paw. Wulf jerked back and scooped up a cloak draped over another stool. "Excuse me," was all he said in a tight voice, and then he was gone in a swirl of black fabric as the cloak settled across his shoulders like a raven unfurling its wings.

How very odd...

Ella picked up the poster of Rooster. "Well, I guess at least we can rule out this fellow." She sighed. That pointed back to Willow and her diabolical poodle. Ridiculous as it sounded.

Ella stared at the heavy oak door that Wulf had stormed out of.

"Are you okay, Ella?" Tomcat said. He blinked his green feline eyes and peered up at her.

"Why wouldn't I be?" She neatly folded the paper and tucked it into her cloak, while feeling around the pocket lining for some coins to leave for the drinks. No, she only had Tom's letter. Argh! She could have asked Wulf to deliver it to Nottingham; he'd be back there in a day or two, no doubt. Foolish old woman, that was a wasted opportunity.

"That man..."

"Prince John's bodyguard. Oh no, you probably don't remember, do you? You were quite unwell when we first encountered him last month." She collected the glasses and placed them in the to-be-washed tray.

"Didn't you see?"

"See what?" Ella returned the whiskey underneath the bar and found a cloth to wipe the counter. "The bite scar? What of it? I expect he's got a few scars hidden across that manly physique..." She idly wiped the cloth across the polished wood before giving herself a mental shake. Magic preserve, was he wearing some magical charm, perhaps? Some item to cast a glamour? That would explain her reaction to his dreaminess...

She sighed, cupped her chin in her palm and leaned against the bar. What was a little age difference after all? It was just a number... Tomcat waved his paws in front of her face, and she jerked back. "Lawks, what? What did you say?"

"I said, not the scar, the tattoo! The three dots on his thumb!"

"No, I didn't." Ella looked around for a scrap of paper so she could leave an IOU to cover the drinks. "What of it?"

"It's a Nottingham prison tattoo!" Tomcat exclaimed, hackles raised. "Hello! He's not a bodyguard. He *is* an escaped prisoner!"

CHAPTER 17

MARTHA'S HUMBLE KITCHEN

CHELTON BUTCHERY, SOUTHGATE SQUARE, CHARMINGTON.

"That can't be right." Ella tore off a corner of Rooster's wanted poster and found a piece of chalk to write out an IOU to leave for Hansel and Gretel. "He said he was chasing after a prisoner..."

"Chasing? He is the prisoner!"

"You must have been mistaken." Ella tapped the chalk against her lips. "Wulf is Prince John's bodyguard—he was there at the archery contest last month." She popped the IOU under a skull beside the novelty cups shaped like fat-bellied dwarves. "Are you sure it wasn't dirt?"

"I know what I saw!" Tomcat insisted, pacing back and forth across the bar top, his claws clicking against the surface. "I used to go with Master Spicer to deliver meals to the prison on Pauper's Day. Each dot represents a decade—that's a thirty-year sentence!"

Ella cast one last look over the bar to ensure everything was tidy and then gathered up her walking stick. "So the question is, has Wulf been sentenced to thirty years since last month? That would incentivise some to make a run for it."

"This isn't a joking matter—Oh! *Or* was he already serving the sentence?" Tomcat beckoned Ella to come closer with a fluffy paw. "There is a rumour," he whispered.

"Why are you whispering?" Ella said. "There's no one else here."

Tomcat held up a warning paw to hush her. "Because it's dangerous to say out loud!"

Ella narrowed her eyes but leaned in close to humour him.

"There's a rumour," Tomcat whispered again, casting a covert glance over his shoulder, "that Prince John has some kind of brutal secret police. Dangerous people recruited from his prisons."

Ella arched an eyebrow. Certainly, Wulf had that sort of vibe. Not the brutal part, but definitely dangerous.

Ella answered back, "Anyway, rumours aside, you burst in here before. Is something happening outside?"

NOTHING WAS HAPPENING OUTSIDE NOW. Due to the fact Bron and the mob had come to an agreement whereby Bron would go quietly and chain himself up in Market Square.

Ella was reliably informed of this by Martha, the butcher's wife, when Ella and Tom ventured outside and stood peering through a window into the empty bakery.

"Don't fret none, my love has gone as his second," Martha assured. "Chelton won't let no one throw fruit and such at Master Bron. And if he hasn't turned into raving werebeast by ten o'clock at latest, well, it's all home to bed and no more said of it."

They were joined at that moment by Marge the midwife, all decked out in her official garb, red cloak, white bonnet, and carrying a willow basket. Her bubbly smile fell away on realising the bakery was closed. "Ugh! Now what? I have to drag myself all the way to the gold fields this afternoon—those dwarves breed like rabbits up there—and Miss Robinne has taken it upon herself to ban me from the Crossroads tavern, where I'd usually stop for a bite to eat."

"Banned you?" Ella voiced, knowing she would regret the answer, but finding herself asking just the same. "What did you do?"

"Me? Nothing at all. I merely told Miss High-and-mighty that she had no right to wear a red cloak, that it was misleading and false advertising. She, not being a trained and professionally authorised midwife."

Martha, sucking on her pipe, adjusted her shawl and said, "I was just about to serve my love his lunch when yon mob arrived. Come inside, you to your ladyship, if you'd honour me. Can't let fresh bacon and egg pie go to waste. You can take a large slice to tide you over, Miss Marge."

"That is kind—I can't stand the dwarven food up at the gold fields." Marge pulled a face. "Always so gritty! And that weird spice they use."

"But as for Robinne, the red cloak was her mother Yara's," Ella felt the need to explain, "and Yara was a midwife."

"Yara? I never heard of her. I took over old mother Goodie's business. She never mentioned anyone called Yara."

"It was well before you came here. Yara worked during the magical black fever outbreak, years back. She were a good lass."

"Indeed, they were dark times. Magic misused creates a lot of mischief and suffering," Ella said as Martha welcomed them into her snug warm little home and bustled about setting cutlery on her scrubbed-clean table. "I can nearly understand why they banned it."

"Magic should be stamped out in the cradle!" Marge added. "I can't stand witches and the like. Horrible creatures."

"Why don't I wrap this pie for thee?" Martha said suddenly, a tight, fixed smile on her face. "Wouldn't want to delay; thee might get stuck out in the woods after dark. With the wolves."

"A very good point!" Marge said, standing up and tying her bonnet back on. "I wouldn't go at all but for how well they pay—ugh! The things we do out of the kindness of our hearts. Lady Ella, will I see you again at the book club next month?"

"Umm, I hadn't thought about it." Ella folded her gloves on her lap and sighed. The tragedy of Arthur's death had left a sour memory on Book Club.

"Do say you will, it's so nice to have a meeting of peers. I would invite you, Martha, of course, but it's the twins' club really, and they are a bit snooty, between you and me, which is odd because they are in trade!"

"Bless your kind heart," Martha replied with fake sincerity, tucking a cloth-wrapped pie into Marge's basket. "If only everyone had such generosity and sympathy for us poor working classes."

A moment later, when the midwife had departed and the peace Marge had disrupted had returned once more, Ella asked, "The twins already invited you and you said, no thanks?"

"Aye," Martha replied, cutting Ella a generous portion of pie and then turning to Tomcat, who, for once, was curled by the fireside, acting like a regular cat. "Pie, Mr Cat? Yes, I remembers full well you can talk, don't fret none—I can't stand gossip—those that grow up in Hot Cockle Lane have loyalty etched on our bones." She glanced to the doorway Marge had disappeared through. "Be they ever so humble."

"Oh! Yes, please!" Tomcat said, standing up and stretching. "The lasagne you made last month was amazing!"

"Get thyself up on a chair, then," Martha added, chuckling at the flattery, gesturing to the seat Marge had left vacant.

"Will Cheapcuts be joining us?" Ella said, asking after the Chelton's son, while tying a napkin around Tomcat's neck. "I wanted to thank him again for the assistance he offered us last month."

Martha shook her head as she lifted the copper kettle from the fire and poured hot water into a pretty little ceramic teapot shaped like a thatched cottage. Martha had a collection of novelty teapots lining the mantel about her kitchen stove. "Making deliveries, bless his heart, he is a kind, hardworking lad." Martha popped the lid on the teapot and repeatedly wiped her hands on her apron, apparently lost in thought. Her eyes darted to several letters tucked in between her castle-shaped teapot and one shaped like a lady's boot. "I hate to be the bearer of bad news, but have ye heard about poor Arthur? I knows he were a good friend of thine." She took plates from the warming drawer of her woodstove oven and loaded them with large portions of her home-cooked pie.

"Indeed, I have, magic rest his soul," Ella replied, taking the offered plate. "How did you find out?"

"That young guardswoman, Miss Turpin, came asked my Chelton for to have a look over the happenings. For his expert opinion and all."

Ella shuddered. That was sensible of Miss Turpin calling in the local butcher, the next best 'bite expert' when Hansel was out of town. She'd been right in thinking the lass would investigate properly.

"It's sad, very sad." Martha pushed a morsel of pie around her plate and sighed. "To think if Arthur hadn't changed his mind about selling the Gatehouse, he might already be spending his retirement on a beach. He'd be gone, but still be with us..."

"What? Arthur *really* planned to sell his business? When? What changed his mind?"

"I don't know the particulars around the sale, but it was the day after the archery contest. I remember it clearly because I had gone to make deliveries and saw Arthur quite shaken, and he said, 'Martha, I have been given a sign that I must not sell. Yesterday, at the contest, I saw a ghost.'"

"A ghost?" Tomcat blurted, pausing from gnawing his pie face-first.

"Aye, his words exactly, a ghost, and he ripped up the contract in front of my eyes and threw on yon fire in the kitchen—burned with a purple flame." Martha picked up her pepper grinder and sprinkled a little on her dish. "Stuck in my mind, don't mind saying it made me feel uneasy."

Ella exchanged a look with Tomcat. If Arthur had agreed to sell, how much bad feeling could that change of mind have created with the intended purchaser? Enough to kill?

CHAPTER 18

SENSITIVE TOPICS

MARTHA'S KITCHEN, CHELTON BUTCHERY, SOUTHGATE SQUARE, CHARMINGTON.

Ella thought over what Cassidy had revealed about the prospect of the smuggling ring trying to buy a legitimate business close to a gatehouse.

"Do you know who made the offer on Arthur's business?" she asked the butcher's wife.

Martha spooned a mouthful of pie and shook her head. "Can't say as I do, but someone in the mayor's office might well recollect. For sure, the town hall would have drawn up a separate contract over the change of tenant."

Ella nodded thoughtfully. That was a good point, and one Cassidy had probably looked into. All the buildings in Charmington were owned by the crown. Arthur might own his business, but the premises were rented.

"What about around here? Have you or your neighbours been approached to sell up?"

Martha nodded in the direction of the bakery. "Funny you should mention that. Several months ago, the neighbours and my love and I received letters, identical but for one word—theirs saying the writer desired to buy a bakery and ours a butchery—it struck me very odd. I threw mine out, but Ginny replied. Nothing came of it as far as I know."

Ella turned this information over in her mind. Could that offer have something to do with Ginny being enticed away to work in neighbouring Nottingham? "Have you heard from Ginny recently?"

"Poor Ginny! More bad luck!" Martha bit a knuckle as if to suppress a darker thought but then seemed to gather herself. She fetched down the bundle of letters tucked between the novelty teapots, and a copy of the *Nottingham Times*. "There was no job waiting for her in Nottingham—it was all some cruel joke."

Ginny Bron had left her baker husband last month and moved to Nottingham to start a new life working a dream job as a pastry chef. Or so they thought.

"That's awful! Who would do such a thing? And why?"

Martha shrugged. "Makes no sense. I saw the advertisements in the *Times* myself—they are still there! Bought a copy today to check." She laid out the paper and found the advert in the back section to show them.

> *Talented bakers sought—Nottingham Palace—excellent wages—apply now! Write care of PO box 99*

"What's Ginny going to do?" Tom asked. "Will she come back here?"

Martha tutted. "No, I don't think so." Her gaze flitted in the direction of the neighbouring bakery, and Ella understood the unspoken hesitation. Ginny and Bron's split had not been amicable. "Fortunately, she's staying with a cousin. She did mention going all the way home to Constantinople, where she and Yara came from originally—but she hasn't been there in what, over ten years?"

"My sister Arabella works for Constantinople's sultan. I will write to her. There's bound to be jobs going for hardworking and talented bakers like Ginny—I think we can both agree Bron's herb-crusted sourdough has been rather stodgy since she left. I'm not saying he was taking credit for her work, but..."

"Aye, that's a fine idea." Martha's eyes kept darting to Tomcat. "Very neighbourly of you."

"Is anything else wrong?" Ella asked.

Martha swallowed.

Ella didn't press. Martha had always been a private woman.

At last, after pouring the tea into pretty tea cups decorated with the coronation of Ella's late father, Martha came to her own decision. "Your Ladyship, since I have your ear, I wanted to ask your advice. 'Tis a matter of a sensitive nature."

"Magic?"

"Aye. And I know full well magic has caused us both heartache, but, well, the thing is, my great granny had a touch of the other."

"A witch?"

"She weren't never so grand as what you'd call a witch. She could read the tea leaves, knew how to make a few charms. Small things. Only, well...you know how it tends to travel down the family...?"

"Cheapcuts!" Ella blurted, quite surprised, nearly upsetting her cup of tea. "Really? I would never have guessed—no offence."

"None taken. I didn't realise it meself for a long time. He were always in his own little world, odd some would say, but anyway, yes, I'm just going to say it." She took a breath and stirred three spoonfuls of sugar into her cup. "He can talk to squirrels. And rabbits. Well, most animals really. T'aint good for a butcher's boy! Poor lad." She glanced at Tom and then back to Ella. "I thought of anyone, you'd understand."

"Indeed!" Ella exclaimed as Tomcat ducked his head with apparent embarrassment. "Have you thought about sending Cheapcuts away to a school so he can learn to channel his powers? There's one in Camelot."

"Bless your heart." Martha wrung her apron between her hands, her face flushed. "But I don't think they take common folks—and anyways, their fees."

"Couldn't you teach him, Ella?" Tomcat said, butting her elbow with his head.

Martha's eyes lit up just as Ella's heart sank. "Without my wand... I'd be about as much use as a fish in a fishing net trying to teach other fish how to swim. I'm sorry."

"Can't be helped." Martha swallowed and smoothed her apron across her lap. "Nothing to be sorry about."

Ella drummed her fingers on the tablecloth. She hated seeing Martha so distressed. There must be something she could do? "In days gone by, I'd suggest he be apprenticed to a craftsman..." Her thoughts drifted to Ace. Despite the ban, Ace clearly dabbled in the craft of magic. Perhaps she could go and have a private word with him?

And if not... "My brother Merlin is on the Camelot school board. I will write to him and find out if there are scholarships. Don't give up hope yet."

CHAPTER 19

CRY WOLF

NORTHGATE SQUARE, CHARMINGTON.

Goodness, to think Cheapcuts could talk to animals—just like her sister Cinderella. No wonder the lad hadn't been surprised by Tom talking last month...

Ella mulled over her conversation with Martha as she walked towards the town hall, where she hoped to access the records room to look over any change of tenancy documents that might have been drawn up for Arthur's building.

Ella had managed to convince Tom to wait behind at the butcher's, under the pretence that a cat wouldn't be allowed within the town hall chambers. While this was certainly true for most people, Ella acknowledged there was a bias towards her with people who wanted to curry favour with the queen, and they probably wouldn't bar her entry should she bring along a tiger on a string. Regardless, keeping Tom out of the way of public officials was for his own good. Imagine if Harold Harper found out Ella had a talking cat? He would cause trouble, never mind who her sister was...

The town hall cluckoo clock was striking four o'clock as Ella reached the square. Dirk Turpin, the royal coachman, at the foot of the town hall steps, was attaching nose bags to the royal coach horses Perry and Peach.

"Long day?" Ella enquired, stroking Perry's mane as the white horses munched away on the feed.

"Aye, ma'am," Dirk answered, indicating over his shoulder at the town hall where a sign had been placed across the twin doors' entrance, closing the hall to public access. "Rental negotiating time. The queen has been in talks with the business association all morning."

Ella frowned. That would definitely interfere with her plans to venture into the records room. She might even have to come back tomorrow.

Hillary Harper, the young girl from the post office, caught Ella's eye. She was sitting on the steps in the sunshine, eating sandwiches, and occasionally breaking off a corner of thin white bread to share with a bold pigeon. Perhaps she was having a late lunch break? Would she have access to the records room? The town hall and post office shared a basement level.

"Behold..." a voice boomed from nearby at the unicorn fountain where a crowd was gathering, and Ella's attention was distracted from the somewhat forlorn figure of the girl eating alone but for the company of a bird.

"...behold the Pipe of Power," Van Helsing announced, drawing out the short black flute Ella had seen the night before. "This pipe was given to me by the sultan of Constantinople himself. It holds powerful magical properties!"

Ella just rolled her eyes.

"Magic is banned," someone coughed from the onlookers. Mr Beau, the shoeshine man. His mouth was partly covered with a filthy polishing cloth stained with brown boot polish as if to disguise his comment. "Just saying."

Van Helsing persisted. "As I said, powerful *natural* properties that can both *reveal* and *disable* those afflicted with the curse of the werebeast's bite. Behold! Listen!" He placed the pipes to his lips, and all eyes followed, but he didn't play. Instead, he waited.

Ella had to give him credit, he had a certain dramatic flair.

The pipe was withdrawn. "Know ye this—all who hear these pipes! Only those of pure heart can hear their sweet music!"

He placed the black pipe to his mouth again and blew.

—toot—parple—squeeeeek

"Oh, good gracious," Ella muttered under her breath. Gretel was right. The man should invest in some music lessons. He was dreadful.

"Do you hear it?" Van Helsing cried out. He pointed to Tobias, who started and dropped his copy of *The Guide*. "Say, ye man—hear you only the sweetest music? Or does the *werebeast's* curse lurk hidden within *your* breast and condemn *your* ears and *your* fate?"

Tobias swallowed. Shuffled. "Ahem. Er... Yes, quite, ahem, melodious."

Others in the audience mirrored his awkward shuffle. Looked at their feet. Someone called out, "Um... can you play again? I wasn't listening."

—toot—toot—squeeeeek!!

"Oh, yes. Very nice." The enquirer had the good grace to look abashed when adding, "I could listen all day."

"Me too!" Mr Beau the bootshine man chirped, while slower brains began to weigh the pros and cons of the situation, and neighbour regarded neighbour with suspicion.

Van Helsing smiled. A wolf among the sheep. "Of course, good citizens, if you command I play all day, all night, I am at your service." He tapped a begging bowl on the edge of the fountain with his boot. "For a modest fee."

The flock of spectators muttered, nudged each other and fidgeted.

He's losing them, Ella thought as she edged nearer, threading her way through the crowd.

"And with me to protect you," Van Helsing continued as if he hadn't noticed the change in the air, "you may sleep sound at night knowing no werebeast may breach these walls. A small price to pay, wouldn't you agree?"

Frowns deepened across the brows of already sceptical faces. Arms were crossed. "How do we know it works?"

It was Ella's turn to grin wolfishly. Maybe the townsfolk weren't so gullible after all.

The busker held aloft his pipe again, high so everyone might see. It didn't look powerful. About a foot long, a line of holes drilled down its length. A glossy black coating was all that set it apart from any homemade shepherd's pipe made from the leg bone of a sheep or something. "Here is proof. Put your hand up if when I played you heard but a discordant noise, a sound that grated your ear bones!" He scanned the onlookers.

A child raised their hand, but a mother snatched it and pinned the child's arm to their side, quickly saying, "Such a mischievous streak, this one. I'm taking you home for your pa to deal with you." And hauled the confused child away.

"As I was saying, a modest fee for a job well done."

"How much?" someone ventured, a bawling babe tucked in the crook of her arm. Mistress Fairweather.

Van Helsing grinned. My, he had big white teeth. "One hundred gold coins."

That broke the spell. "But that's two years' wages!"

Tobias wasn't the only one to baulk, and the crowd started to murmur and break up when—

Ooowwooowwwooo!

Even Ella was caught off guard. The eerie howl ripped through the square, echoing off stone walls.

The citizens gasped and gawked at each other. Where had it come from?

"Sounded like blackest grief," Mr Beau the bootshine man croaked, polishing cloth clutched to his chest, "like having your heart ripped out."

"Aye, like yer soul being torn apart!" another voiced to a muttered chorus of agreement.

For a moment, Ella was caught up in the fear and confusion until her common sense overrode the initial surprise.

How very cunning. How very well-timed. How ever did he manage that? He must have signalled some cohort nearby.

She shaded her eyes and peered over to the furthest recesses of the buildings and town wall. A patrol of guards inspecting a loaded cart at the north gate had stopped in their business and were likewise looking this way and that.

Indeed, where had the howl come from?

She turned and sought out Van Helsing's face from the milling crowd. He was pale.

"Well done," Ella murmured, restraining herself from clapping at the show. Indeed, here was a first-class actor as good as any travelling troupe performing the annual All Hallows' eve play or the Pickford Players' Christmas production of Joan of Arc.

Ooowwwooowww!

Van Helsing gulped, stepped down from his fountain-side pulpit and tried to elbow through the crowd. Blocked by the very wall of citizens that had formed watching him, he was forced back up onto the fountain's edge to stand out slightly above everyone else. He cast nervous glances over his shoulder and repeatedly turned about as if trying to locate the howl's origin.

Odd. He genuinely looked scared. Was this *not* part of the show?

Hillary screamed. She jumped to her feet. Egg sandwiches scattered onto the town hall steps. Heads turned, following her shaking fingertip. Hillary pointed to the private dining room window of the Gatehouse Inn that protruded out above the square. "W–wwwo–wolf!"

"What?"

Several things happened at once.

The window blew out as the biggest, blackest wolf Ella had ever seen burst through the panes. Raining glass on the cobbles, the beast launched itself at the unicorn fountain.

The crowd screamed, and everyone ran. All directions, colliding, panicking. *Get away! Get away!* the collective instinct of the moment.

"Son of a witch!" Van Helsing swore, standing stock still. Until a second later, survival instinct kicked in, and he flung his arms over his face and ducked. The snarling beast clamped its salivating jaws onto the back of Van Helsing's rotting sheepskin jerkin, sending both busker and wolf crashing and skidding across the frozen surface of the fountain.

In the citizens' panic, Ella was knocked from her feet. She landed on top of Mr Beau, the boot shiner, in a gust of turpentine air, mere feet from the fountain.

"Help me!" Van Helsing wailed, on his belly, clawing at his pipe, fallen inches from his grasp. The giant wolf regained its footing, black claws clicking on the ice, pink tongue lolling, sharp white canines dripping saliva.

My, what big teeth. What black fur. The eyes so brown, they could be black.

Over the right eye, the black fur was streaked with white.

A white streak?

And around its foreleg, a silver manacle.

Oh dear.

The recognition jolted Ella like a slap. She struggled to her feet, only to be knocked over again by more fleeing townspeople.

"Help me!" Fingers brushed the black flute and grabbed it. Van Helsing rolled onto his back as the wolf snapped its jaws and leapt.

Pipe set to his lips, Van Helsing blew.

—*toot—parple*—

The black wolf's whole body convulsed like a jolt of lightning had struck it mid-flight. It yelped. It plummeted. Huge muscular legs gave way and it crashed onto the solid ice.

Magic preserve! Did the pipe actually work? Ella pushed her hair back from her eyes as Van Helsing, still prone like a beetle on his back, blew with all his might.

—-*squeeekkkk!!!*—

The black wolf writhed, pawed at its ears, howled and thrashed as if in terrible, limb-rendering pain. Somehow, it flipped itself upright and, scrabbling claws against the ice, it fled. Pounded away across the cobbles—barrelling straight for the cart blocking the north gate. Guards and carter alike scattered as the beast launched itself across the cart, sailing over the donkey that bellowed and reared in panic, tipping the cart and goods. Black paws touched down. Thundered across the drawbridge and was gone in a heartbeat.

Van Helsing collapsed back onto the fountain, chest heaving in exertion, sweat drenching his brow, the flute clutched to his breast like sweet life itself.

A steady hand clamped onto Ella's elbow, and Dirk Turpin pulled her upright. "Ma'am, are you hurt? Speak to me," Dirk asked of Ella, but too stunned to talk, she could only nod as the chaos roiled around her in waves of confusion and grief, like when she was a child and an avalanche had swept her parents and their hunting party down the side of the mountain, leaving her staring at nothing. She cast her horrified gaze to the north gate and the dark shrouding cover of the forest beyond where the black wolf with the white streak had vanished.

"Magic preserve!"

Charmington did have a werewolf. And she knew who.

CHAPTER 20

THE QUEEN'S ENTRANCE
AND VAN HELSING'S EXIT

"Shut the gates! Shut the gates!"

Ella turned away from the town guards running to action. The buildings seemed to sway and loom above her, and she wobbled. "I need to sit," she told Dirk, who was still supporting her arm.

"Yes, yes, allow me." He immediately stripped off his purple frock coat and folded it across the town hall steps. "Please, ma'am, I've got you. There you go." He assisted her to a sitting position, and she laced her fingers together over the top of her walking stick as she breathed deeply to calm her racing heart and gather her wits.

"We are all doomed!" Mistress Fairweather wailed, doing a fair job of teaching by example, her lung capacity nearly outshining her crying babe. "We shall be eaten alive in our beds!"

Hillary, who had spotted the wolf, though pale of face and looking like she might throw up, was conscientiously picking up all the discarded sandwiches from the steps.

Nearby, her father, Postmaster Harold Harper, peered cautiously around the great oak door of the post office. "Come along, Hillary, leave that! Your tea break was over five minutes ago!" He flapped his hands, slapping at anyone who thought to seek shelter in the building. "Keep out! The post office is closed for urgent repairs! Hillary, leave it!" His eyes caught Ella's, and he glared as if to say, *'I don't know how, but I know this is all your fault!'*

Ella sniffed and looked away. Horrid man. But he wasn't her problem, not today. He would keep. She had far greater problems than his hurt feelings.

Wulf. A werewolf. What did it all mean? Did Prince John know? And worst of all, had Wulf killed Arthur?

"Are you all right, ma'am, if I leave you for a moment?" Dirk said, rubbing his arms to keep warm and shivering in his shirtsleeves. "I must attend the coach." He pointed to an alley where Peach and Perry had bolted.

Ella bid the coachman go, wishing him all the best for the state of his two horses.

"I ate there *yesterday!*" A large woman, all curves and curls, dressed in a figure-hugging white outfit with a matching fur-trimmed cape, who had draped herself across the steps a short distance away, was crying, "Woe! Oh, woe! What is to become of *meee*?" Her bosom heaved as Tobias used his copy of *The Guide* to fan her.

What was her name? Oh, yes, Nigella Pickford. Ella recognised the amateur dramatics having seen Pickford's Players perform on several occasions at the Crossroads tavern's mid-winter variety show. Nigella made a marvellous Joan of Arc soliloquy last year, leaving no dry eyes in the tavern when she was led off for execution.

Mistress Fairweather didn't seem to appreciate the lack of attention and cried out, "Arthur, a werewolf! How could we not know?" This was met with much head nodding and grumbles of disquiet.

Ella blinked. How had the citizens jumped to that misguided conclusion? She peered over to where she'd last seen Van Helsing. He was still at the fountain, investigating the hole torn in the back of his jerkin and complaining loudly about the costs of having to maintain his equipment.

At that moment, a large gathering of the town's business owners spilled out from the ornately carved twin doors of the town hall. The rental meeting that had been occupying Queen Sibylla must finally be over.

Sibylla, dressed in a white fox fur cloak over a purple silk gown, with an elegantly understated golden circlet nestled atop her lustrous chestnut locks, appeared at the top of the steps in conversation with the doddering elderly mayor, and another younger man bearing a copy of the mayor's beakish nose to seal the family resemblance. They were quickly surrounded by an entourage of ladies-in-waiting, officials, palace guards and the more important members of the business community, including the haberdashery owners, Millie and Sally, who were wearing matching coats in bright canary yellow, and on seeing Ella sitting in the frosted steps, rushed down to offer their aid.

"Lady Ella!" cried Sally, extracting a sandalwood folding fan from her purse. She fluttered it across Ella's face, asking, "Did you faint? You look like you've seen a ghost!"

"Whatever has been going on out here?" echoed Millie, as the palace and business officials slowed their procession as, collectively, they came to the realisation it wasn't their grand presence that was currently the talk on everyone's lips.

An uneasy silence settled over the square.

"What is the meaning of this?" Sibylla demanded, casting her royal gaze on her gathered people and beyond to the far gates, which were now bolted and lined with guards armed with crossbows and peering out over the city wall to the forest. "The gates, barred? I did not order that. Open them at once!"

"Arthur has turned into a werewolf!" Nigella Pickford the actress boomed in her clear stage voice, on her feet in an instant. "No one is safe!" And seeing all eyes were on her, she placed a languid hand to her brow and, in the performance of a lifetime, rocked back off the steps and swooned into Tobias and Mr Beau's arms, who gallantly struggled between them to bear her weight.

"It shouldn't be allowed!" Mistress Fairweather shouted angrily, and then immediately aghast, bobbed a succession of curtseys as if sheer numbers might make up for her daring to scold the queen.

Van Helsing, suitably recovered from his ordeal, ventured up the steps, stopped a respectable distance away and, with a hand-waving flourish that Nigella would have approved had she not still been pretending to be passed out in the arms of the schoolmaster and shoe shiner, bowed low. "Majesty, if I might be so bold as to introduce myself..."

Bolder still, the cloud of rancid mutton that hung about the busker made itself known first. Sibylla and her ladies-in-waiting gagged and covered their noses before a palace guard took it upon himself to usher the busker further away with the sharp end of his ceremonial pike.

"Wait!" squeaked Van Helsing, rattling his rat skull necklace, which it's fair to say didn't improve the less-than-hygienic impression he was making, "I can help—see, no wait, here! The Pipe of Power!"

"Aye, 'tis true," Mistress Fairweather vouched, and the gathered people nodded and murmured general agreement, "we all saw it! His wretched—I mean, the beautiful—well, anyway, the *noise* he made drove the savage beast off!"

"What savage beast?"

"The werebeast hiding among—" Van Helsing began, then flinched as the palace guard gripped his pike threateningly.

"Arthur! Arthur has turned into a werewolf," Tobias shouted, picking up his copy of *The Guide* again and leaving Mr Beau to struggle with Nigella Pickford's womanly physique by himself. "The guards have lied to us; Arthur isn't dead—he's a werewolf! It's the only logical explanation." The school teacher turned to his fellow citizens for support.

"And *his* pipe saved us!" Nigella Pickford trilled, levering herself upright as the fleeting spotlight that is public attention drifted near her again. "That smelly man saved us all!"

"My name is Van Helsing, Your Majesty. Supernatural exterminator, at your service."

During this odd exchange, Sibylla remained quiet. Only now her shrewd gaze turned to Ella. "Is this true?"

All eyes regarded Ella, and she rose to her feet with Millie and Sally's assistance. "There was a large *wolf*," she put emphasis on the word, "and yes. Van Helsing's *noise* drove it off." She crossed her arms. "That much is true."

Sibylla regarded Ella coldly for a moment, and then, addressing the palace guard hovering beside Van Helsing, snapped, "Arrest that man. Confiscate his pipe."

Van Helsing's mouth dropped open. "But Your Majesty! I must protest! Only I can play the Pipe of Power!"

The guard flexed as if bracing to elbow the busker in the stomach, but Van Helsing saw it coming, ducked and made a break for it. Dashing off down the nearest alley with cries of "Catch that man!" and various guards and enterprising townspeople chasing after him.

Sibylla's trademark lip curl of disgust appeared momentarily, but then she turned away, and, in a rustle of skirts, her ladies-in-waiting enveloped her in a fashionable cocoon of silk taffeta as the entourage followed its mistress, and no one spared Ella another glance.

"But the rent increases!" Millie cried despairingly as if there were more important things than stray wolves and runaway buskers, and she trailed after the court. Sally bobbed a curtsy to Ella and then hurried after her sister.

CHAPTER 21

THE FORGOTTEN ACADEMY

EAST AVENUE, HAVERSHAM ACADEMY, CHARMINGTON.

Ella met up with Tom on the corner of East Avenue and Main Street, where Tomcat waited at the foot of a bronze statue of her brother Merlin that had been erected many years ago.

Someone had painted a moustache on the statue. Very recently. The red paint was slowly dripping off the statue's chin.

A few buildings away, Ella spied the three jumper-wearing orphan children whom Tom had played with a few hours earlier at the unicorn fountain. One of them hid something behind his back—a pot of jam, it looked like—while the others giggled.

Shouldn't they be in school? Perhaps she would have a word with Master Tobias. Then again, it wasn't her nature to interfere.

"I'm sorry, what did you say?" Ella asked as Tom fell into step with her and began talking enthusiastically, his whiskers fanning in delight.

"I was saying," Tomcat said, "that East Avenue is my favourite street in all of Charmington!"

It had been many years since Ella had walked down the wide, tree-lined boulevard of elegant townhouses that made up most of East Avenue, but she could still see the attraction. And though the once lush cherry trees were now stripped bare in the grip of eternal winter, the street remained the most fashionable address in Charmington. She glanced up back at the castle, from where in her former East tower bed chambers she had had a spectacular view down the grand street, and from where she had spent many an hour watching the comings and goings of the ladies and gentlemen who strolled or rolled in open-top carriages along the white-cobbled street. And once every week, she had walked to Mrs Haversham's academy, one of her favourite places in Charmington.

"Aren't you going to ask *why* it's my favourite?" Tomcat grinned as he padded along, weaving in and out of the trees.

"*Why* is East Avenue your favourite?" Ella asked with good humour.

"I met Cassidy here." He leapt up onto one of the many wrought-iron bench seats nestled among the line of cherry trees. "Right there, under that streetlamp." A white paw gestured to a streetlamp that looked the same as all the others. "It was my first night as a guard, and I was too excited to sleep, so I went for a walk, and there she was, her knee pressed into the spine of some cutpurse she was trying to arrest, and I rushed over to offer assistance." Tomcat sighed lovingly. His grin only widened as he recalled the memory. "Do you know what she said?"

Ella just arched an eyebrow, giving him leave to answer.

"She said, 'If I need your blinking help, *Rookie*, I'll blinking well ask for it!'" Tomcat shrugged sheepishly. "Only, er, she didn't say blinking. Ahem."

"No..." Ella imagined a few creative expressions the young guardswoman was more likely to have said in the heat of the moment. "What happened next?" Ella asked kindly, walking on.

"And then!" Tomcat said, trotting to keep up. "The thief knocked her feet out from under her and ran off!" Tomcat rocked back on his heels and laughed at the memory. "And Cassidy yells at me, 'Are you waiting for a blinking invitation! After him!'"

Ella smiled. Clearly, Tom was smitten. To think he'd been a cat now for more weeks than he'd ever been a guard. How much longer might he remain as a cat? Would Cassidy's heart still be available when Tom was human again? Poor lad.

Her mind drifted to memories of her own, to the first time she had met Richard. Both of them had been hunting for fairy lights in the depths of Wyld Enchantment Woods. They had become friends instantly, but just when she thought they might be something more... Richard met Cinderella.

Ella halted, leaning on her walking stick, at the foot of a grand townhouse four stories tall in white-dressed stone. Above the door, a discreet bronze plaque was hung

> *Haversham Academy, Institute for Refinement and Magical Education, by Royal Appointment, EST 1758.*

"What is this place?" Tomcat said, his fur bristling as though some inner sense alerted him to the darkness lurking behind a pleasant facade. Though the building's appearance was as neat and well-maintained as its neighbours, all the windows were shuttered and lifeless.

"It used to be a private school for young ladies."

"I thought we were going to Willow's bakery?"

"The Academy's garden wall backs onto properties on Fifth Street," Ella explained, "and the tea shop Willow took over shares the wall."

"Oh, so we're spying?"

"Spying. Investigating," Ella said with a shrug. "The ends justify the means…" She paused. That had always been Mrs Haversham's favourite expression. She shook off the memory. Once, she had hung on Mrs Haversham's every word. No more.

"This way," she directed, heading for a narrow path between the academy and a neighbouring building. After walking down a few steps, she paused at the tall black iron gate that barred the side entrance to the back garden. The gate was forged to resemble an elaborate thatch of ivy leaves in iron. Now the iron ivy leaves were twined with real ivy that had wrapped its way up the gate. Beyond their view, the garden was choked with a wall of thistles as tall and thick as a plantation of corn. Ella placed a hand on the gate and hissed, jerking her hand back as thorns from rogue rose canes also encroaching the gate jabbed her palm.

Ella tutted and glanced at the shutters and dark arched glass of the basement windows. "Well, we can't go this way into the back garden. We'll have to go through the school itself."

And leaving the ivy and rose cane-choked gate, she walked up to the side entrance. With a darted glance back to the avenue to make sure no one was passing, she clasped the doorknob. The lock clicked as she turned the handle, and the door swung open in a gust of jasmine-scented air.

"Did you know that would be unlocked?" Tomcat said, his bushy tail curling about the door frame. "We'll have to tell someone."

"Mmm," Ella muttered in non-committal agreement while she regarded the hallway before her and blinked in the gloom to get her bearings.

Once, fairy lights set in niches along the walls had illuminated the corridors with a pleasant glow, but now the darkened hall stretched before her like a cave, or worse, a tomb.

Ella tapped her walking stick twice against the tiled floor, and light spilt from the tip, illuminating the entrance area. A brass umbrella stand still had a faded blue parasol, a large looking glass was covered with a light coating of dust and long dead roses drooped from a vase, their petals brittle as egg shells. Along the walls, oil paintings and watercolours were hung, some with sheets over them. It all added to the air of faded grandeur and neglect. The black fever had started here. A magical plague born out of spite.

The black fever had seen an end to the school, and in many ways, an end to Ella's way of life.

Ella swallowed. "East Avenue was once my favourite place too..." she found herself saying softly, before pulling herself together, and she marched down the dim corridor towards the music room that would connect to the conservatory from where they might access the garden.

But on reaching the point where the side entrance hall connected with the grand oak-panelled central hall, Tomcat stopped in his tracks and gawked at a large oil painting of a group of young ladies that was hung next to a large and now silent grandfather cluckoo clock. "Look, it's Queen Sibylla!" Tomcat said, standing on his hind paws to better see the painting in the half-light. "Did she go to school here?" Tomcat looked over his shoulder up at Ella. "She is beautiful when she smiles, don't you think?"

Ella let go of the breath she hadn't consciously been holding as she regarded the painting depicting not Sibylla, but herself and her fellow year of graduating students. Of course, it had never occurred to her, but Tom had only ever seen her as an old woman, and though he knew Sibylla was her sister *and* her twin, she had never thought to mention they were identical. Ella managed to nod. "One wonders how the portrait painter ever got her to smile..."

But Tomcat was studying the portrait again, peering up at the other four young women. "Wow, this girl is the most beautiful person I think I have *ever* seen! Is this depiction accurate. Did you know these ladies?"

Ella shifted her gaze from her own image captured in oil to that of her younger sister. Hair as fair as hers was dark, the blonde tresses flowed in soft round brush strokes. "That is Cinderella." She reached up to trace a curl of golden hair. "And no, it does not do her justice. Cinderella was beauty itself, inside and out..."

Tomcat sat back on his haunches. "You never said how she passed...?"

Ella held her walking stick aloft, directing the pool of light up the oak-panelled wall, across the other paintings until she found the one she'd been looking for. An elaborate gilt frame enclosed a portrait of a proud-looking, older woman. Black-violet eyes, a crown of lustrous black hair swept up into a chignon, and a porcelain complexion that made her ruby lips appear as if they were coated in blood. "Mrs Haversham, headmistress, the school's founder…"

Tomcat gulped. "She looks like she eats small children."

Ella laughed gruffly. It was as apt a description as any. "A powerful witch, she…looked down on those without magical abilities." Ella shook her head and drew a deep breath. "No, that's untrue… The truth is she was a horrible old *bigot*." Ella clenched her teeth as she said the word. "Long story short. She created the black fever. She designed it to kill humans."

Tomcat's mouth dropped open. "Cinderella died of the fever?"

"No, though she had given up her magic to marry Richard, the fever could not harm Cinderella." Ella cast the light over the portrait of her former favourite teacher once more. "I discovered Mrs Haversham was the cause of the fever. I confronted her. Called her out in front of everyone." Ella slowly lowered the light and leaned over the top of the walking stick. "She laughed. *Laughed!* Denied it! And though I knew it was her doing, at the time I could not prove it."

In the stillness Tomcat, did not speak, just waited for her to carry on.

"I kept digging, and in an attempt to shut me up, Haversham poisoned an apple." Ella's light wavered over Cinderella's portrait. Such blue eyes. Cornflower-blue eyes, so full of joy, so full of life. "But the wrong sister ate it."

"That's dreadful, I'm so sorry," Tomcat whispered, his big green eyes limpid with tears.

Ella felt a hot sting flicker in her eyelids, and she turned away and rubbed her sleeve cuff over her face. "Lawks, it is very dusty in here. Come along now, the music room is just beyond the library."

With Tomcat trailing after her, Ella navigated through the dim corridors that were once the centre of her life and full of promise but were now stark and empty and best forgotten.

Chapter 22

Willow's Secret

Garden of Haversham Academy, Charmington.

Though less dark than the hallways, the spacious music room was not as bright as Ella recalled, and the interior was cast in a weird green glow. The grand piano and harp were covered in large white sheets, and dust motes curled in the air as Ella and Tomcat strode past toward the adjoining conservatory and discovered the source of the strangely coloured light.

"Oh, my!" Tomcat breathed as they entered the glassed-in conservatory and a sudden increase in temperature hit them like they had opened an oven door. Tropical plants of all kinds grew thick and tangled, all competing for the sunlight outside beyond the tall, leaded-glass windows. Moisture dripped from the ceiling, and everywhere flowers bloomed and fruit hung like some fabled garden of paradise. "Wow, why is there a jungle in the middle of a Charmington school? Look, are they orchids?" Tomcat disappeared under a verdant rubber plant leaf to pop out a second later next to a banana palm. "Are those really bananas?"

Ella breathed in the thick, stifling air and regarded the burgeoning crop of hanging fruit. "You've never seen a bunch of bananas before?"

He shrugged. "I've never seen them growing on a tree. What is this place, and how come it's so warm in here?"

"It's an orangery, technically," Ella explained, dodging under the palm fronds and watching her footing as the encroaching plants had dislodged many of the floor tiles in their unfettered expansion. "A warm place to grow exotic fruit. The castle is built on thermal vents, and most of the houses along East Avenue are also plumbed in. Warm air, heated water, straight into your house for those who can afford it." Ella paused in front of a hacked-back sugarcane plant. A clear path had been cut to an outside door. "Keep an eye out. We may not be alone."

She opened the side door and stepped outside into the back garden and breathed in the crisp air. The sudden drop in temperature was a welcome reprieve from the weight of the hot school air pressing down on her.

Someone had been busy out in the garden too. Down the crushed-gravel path, the lush herb garden had been pruned back recently. The scent of rosemary and mint hung in the air. And there among the dark green mint bloomed a plant she had only just become familiar with. Ella reached out to touch the purple flowers with the end of her walking stick.

"Wolfsbane?" Tomcat said at her side, peering closely at the plant.

Ella's boot heels rasped on the gravel as she stood and regarded the high stone wall that enclosed the academy garden from its back boundary neighbour. A birdbath built in the shadow of the wall and a thick trail of ivy marked the place where, as a school girl, she had climbed up and over and snuck into the tea garden of Ginger Brewed tea shoppe. The birdbath now sagged against the wall as if someone heavy or clumsy had knocked the bowl over when climbing.

"What are you doing here?"

Ella started on hearing Willow's voice behind the wall, but a moment later, realised the question wasn't directed at her when a second familiar voice answered from the neighbouring garden, "They're chasing me! Ungrateful simpletons."

Van Helsing.

Ella and Tomcat exchanged surprised glances.

Ella tapped a finger to her lips, warning Tomcat to keep quiet.

"Get out of here!" Willow wailed. "You said I wouldn't have to see you again. You *promised*!"

Tomcat was already clawing his way up the ivy-covered back wall before Ella could say, "Go see what's going on."

The argument continued as Ella regarded the toppled birdbath and ivy vines. If she was just a hundred years younger, she'd be over this wall in a trice!

"Quit badgering me, woman—I just need a place to lie low. They'll be desperate to pay me in a day or two and—*Ouch!* What was that for?"

"Get out! Get out!"

There came the distinct noises of Willow's jangling bracelets and someone being repeatedly slapped. Ella dug her fingers into the thick vines and hauled herself up to the top of the wall beside Tomcat. Near out of breath, she peeped into Willow's garden below to see the young woman chase Van Helsing around her small courtyard with a rolled-up newspaper until he retreated out of her side gate. When he was gone, Willow crouched under her clothesline, which was oddly enough covered in dripping wet sheets of the *Nottingham Times*, and flung her arms over her face to muffle her sobs.

Much to Ella's dismay, Tomcat called out, "Willow, are you all right?"

Willow started. Realising she wasn't alone, she glared up at Ella. "Oh, so I see you've discovered my secret! Well, fine!" she cried defiantly and wiped a fist across her eyes. She gestured to her odd washing day line-up of broadsheets. "You want to blackmail me too? Like my wretched ex-husband! Go on, then, tell everyone I'm a witch!"

CHAPTER 22

THE UNDERGROUND SCENE

WILLOW'S BAKERY, THE FORMER GINGER BREWED TEA SHOPPE, FIFTH STREET.

"My dear," began Ella with as much dignity as she could muster while lying prone across the garden wall and aware that one of her boots was caught in the ivy, "even if I knew how washing newspapers made you a witch, I assure you, your secret is safe with me."

"You can totally trust Ella," piped up Tomcat beside her. "She's magical too!"

Ella cast him a despairing look. "The cat, however, is an appalling tattletale."

"What?" Tomcat huffed, sitting back on his fluffy haunches and crossing his paws. "No, I'm not!"

Willow's mouth hung open. "Your cat talks! Properly! Like a person! How is that possible?"

"And I'm not *her* cat," Tom interjected moodily, his tail flicking like a switch.

"Technically, you *are*," Ella rebutted and shuffled awkwardly in the vines, trying to kick her snagged foot free.

"*Technically*, I'm not," Tomcat muttered under his breath while clambering down into Willow's garden via a stack of old tea crates piled like a staircase up against the inside of the wall, which assumedly Willow had arranged for precisely that purpose.

Willow, by this time, had dried her tears. She gawked at Ella, still straddling the wall. "What are you? A witch? Something else? You must be extremely powerful to make your cat talk. I've never heard of such a thing!"

Ella finally yanked her boot free of the vines and hauled herself up over the edge of the wall and tentatively put a toe on the tea chest staircase, but it was remarkably firm underfoot. "I am Fae."

Willow gasped and fell to her knees. "Fae!" she whispered in breathy awe and clapped her hands.

Tomcat's ears flicked up and he threw a confused expression back at Ella as if to say, *What's that about?*

That is proper respect which comes from true understanding of what you're dealing with! is what Ella wanted to say, but on glancing back over the boundary wall onto the academy side where her walking stick lay discarded on the frosty gravel path, she could only sigh. "My dear, would you be so kind as to assist an old woman by popping over and fetching my stick?"

Willow's expression of unadulterated adoration cracked. "Er...why don't you...?" She snapped her fingers meaningfully.

Ella grimaced. "My powers have been bound."

"Oh!" Willow clamped a hand to her mouth. "You poor thing! You poor, *poor* creature!"

AFTER A LITTLE EFFORT, AND much fussing, Ella found herself ensconced in the pleasant and light-filled kitchen of Willow's small bakery, hands clasped around a steaming cup of mint and bergamot tea. Tomcat was peering through the glass door of a large stove that dominated the room, licking his lips and watching a tray of brownies baking with all the dedication that a regular cat might devote to an unwary sparrow splashing about in a bird bath.

Willow, jewellery jangling, pulled out a chair to sit opposite Ella at the kitchen table and slid an old copy of the *Nottingham Times* in front of her. "So, you don't know about the underground scene? Truly?"

Ella could only shrug as she breathed in the chocolatey aroma saturating the warm room. "Truly. Enlighten me."

Willow made a small squeal of delight and started removing several of her bangles and amulets and piling them in a heap at the end of the table. Next, she fetched a mixing bowl and poured hot water from the kettle into the bowl, adding some dried blueberries, all the while muttering something about what an honour it was to show one of the illustrious Fae something new. At last, she took a dry sponge that had been wrung out over the sink, dunked it in the purple-tinged water and then sloshed the soaked sponge across the newspaper.

Ella sat back a little as the water flooded the paper broadsheet when suddenly the sodden text of the news article heading shimmered and changed in front of her eyes.

Prince John, Hero! changed to *Prince John, Hero?*

"Oh. My. Goodness," said Ella, her tone of disbelief breaking through Tom's dedication to his stomach, and he darted up onto the table to read over her shoulder. She caught Willow's eye. "The newspaper is really, what? A covert communication network?"

Willow giggled in glee and nodded enthusiastically. "It's only temporary—soon as it dries, it changes back."

"But why? Magic isn't banned in Nottingham."

Willow looked grim. "No, not yet, but it's increasingly being controlled. There have been...disappearances." She restrung the rose quartz amulets about her neck and threaded the bracelets back on her wrists. Ella noted that all the pieces of jewellery Willow had taken off had either rose or white quartz beads in common.

"Clever." She smiled. "Quartz fractures magical fields." She nodded, impressed. "You're suppressing your powers through dispersion."

"Yes." Willow sighed. She glanced at the back garden visible out the kitchen window beyond the sink. "My ex-husband works for Prince John as an informer. Works in the prison." She clasped her hands in her lap. "When two fortune tellers from my neighbourhood were imprisoned on false charges, I thought I might be next. So I left."

Ella nodded. She remembered the dark days when magic fell out of favour in Charmington. Due to Mrs Haversham's spiteful crime of starting the black fever, people had been looking for something to direct their blame on while they came to terms with the people they had lost. Subsequently, all magic was regarded as evil.

"And what of Mr Puddles?" Willow looked hopeful. "Did you find anything out?"

Ella was about to reveal the conversation with Cassidy when a moment of doubt crossed Ella's mind. Willow seemed kind and genuine...but had she learned nothing from Mrs Haversham's betrayal? And after all, she barely knew Willow...

Instead, Ella patted Willow's hands. "I am working on it. Trust me, I won't let anything bad happen to your poodle."

"Is something burning?" Tomcat cried, leaping off the table and rushing over to the oven.

As Willow went to open the oven door and check on the brownies, Ella drummed her fingernails on the teacup. And just how did Wulf fit into this? Could Tom's suggestion be correct? Was Wulf an escaped prisoner? Certainly, it was Wulf who had attacked Van Helsing while

Van Helsing had only defended himself. And if *instead,* they both worked for Prince John, why would they be fighting? And did either of them have something to do with Arthur's death?"

"Is Van Helsing a werewolf?"

"No!" Willow snorted, setting the piping-hot tray down on the top of the stove, and added in a mutter, "He *wishes* he was a werewolf. Can't believe he'd show up here."

Ella cocked an eyebrow. "Why did you choose Charmington? I would have thought our ban on magic was well known."

Willow shrugged. "It's much closer than Camelot, and when an old friend of Van agreed to sell his share of this business to me at a bargain rate, it seemed too good an opportunity to miss. I should have known there was a catch."

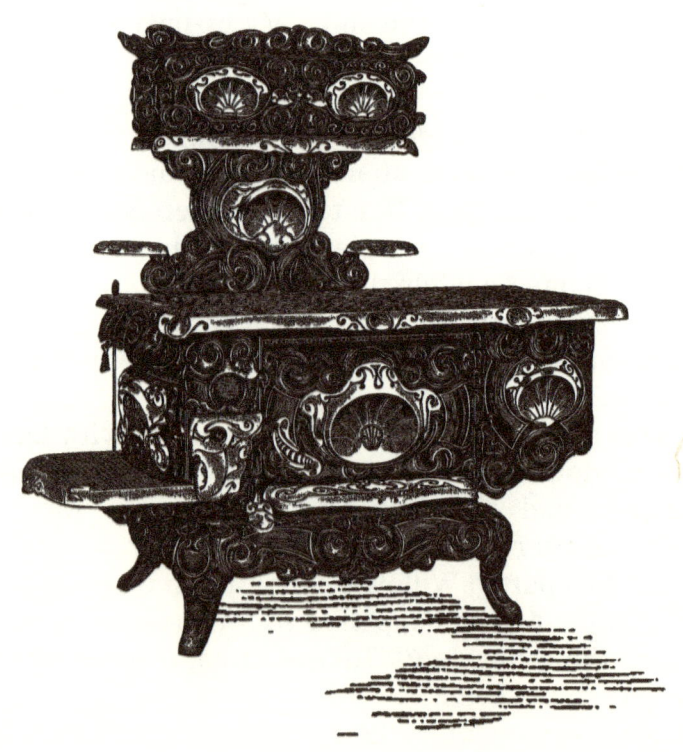

Chapter 24

The Tinker and the Thief

Old Road, Wyld Enchantment Woods.

Walking stick in hand, Ella trekked the snow-covered forest path, occasionally slowing as the dappled sunlight changed the ground from white to deep blue in the shadows of the fir trees, but otherwise trusting her feet to find the path home as they had done for many years. Scampering ahead, Tomcat darted from one pool of sunlight to the next. His fleeting attention was drawn by chattering squirrels, fresh rabbit tracks, and interestingly shaped rocks.

It had been a long strange day, and the thoughts of everything she'd seen and learned weighed on her. Arthur's plan to sell his business was as shocking as his death. He had been a fixture in her life for so long. If he was unhappy here, why wouldn't he have told her? Perhaps it was her own fault. She had withdrawn into herself, living out in the forest. She wasn't too proud to acknowledge that if it hadn't been for Tom's blundering into her life and pushing her to mix again with the Charmington folks, she would have missed the chance to rekindle her friendship with Arthur.

"Listen!" Tomcat exclaimed, pausing at the base of a gnarled old oak. "Bells! Is it the queen's carriage?"

Ella leaned on her walking stick while listening to the hollow rattle of what sounded more like an old goat bell than the shimmering silver bells that accompanied the queen's coach. She peered around the other side of the wide oak to discover the source of the sound. A fat, rather old mule, trailing a broken lead, was nosing at tree roots and nibbling a scattering of acorns. A brass bell was tied about his neck. "Isn't this tinker Potts' mule?" Ella said, gathering up the rope, and she scratched the beast between his long ears. "Goodness, where is Mr Potts?" She examined the end of the frayed rope. "Chewed through."

Tomcat cocked an ear and jabbed a paw at a cluster of Hawthorn bushes further off the path. "There's someone in there!"

Ella strained her ears and held her breath. In the still of the forest, the birdsong fell silent. "Hee hee! My lucky day!" came the sound of someone talking to themselves beyond the cover of the bushes. A familiar someone.

"Marge!" Ella muttered, and, guiding the mule after her, she ventured deeper off the path to a small but sheltered campsite favoured by travellers and peddlers caught out in the forest overnight.

The tinker's camp was in disarray, frying pans and pots were strewn everywhere, the tent stood but was saggy and lopsided, and the fire was long dead. Marge the midwife stood over Mr Potts, who lay curled up in a tight ball, cradling to his chest a large copper stock pot. Marge was trying to free the pot from his rictus grasp.

Marge looked up and scowled. "I found him first, so the stock pot is mine, but you can help yourself to the frying pans."

Ella blinked in horror, managing to compose herself long enough to tie the mule's lead to a branch. "You're robbing the dead!"

Marge snorted and placed her hands on her hips. "It's not like *I* killed him!" She gestured to the blackened fire pit and then to the tinker's grimacing face, which was covered with a coating of frost. "Clearly, he froze to death. Silly fool. Now, are you going to help me with this? Sweet mercy, his grip on this pot!" She bent down again and tugged at the dead tinker's elbow.

Tomcat's fur suddenly stood up on end. "Wait! Can't you hear it? A scratching noise!"

Marge was so intent on her purpose that she didn't seem to notice Tom had spoken, but she withdrew her hand sharply. "That's odd... Is there something inside the pot?"

Tink Tink Ting

Marge grinned and yanked again at the poor frozen corpse. "Oh! What treasure are you hiding, little man?" With a grunt of satisfaction, she pried the clutched stock pot loose, revealing Mr Pott's bloodstained shirt and chest had been ripped to shreds.

"Wait!" Ella cried as the realisation struck her. Mr Potts hadn't just frozen to death, he had died trying to keep something from getting out of that pot. Something terrible. "Marge, get away!" Ella fumbled with her walking stick. Magic preserve, the hidden dagger! Which button released the blade?

A black rat's oily head peered over the lip of the copper pot. Its nose twitched, smelling the air. It blinked little red eyes.

Marge leaned down to tip the rat out.

The rat's intense red eyes *glowed*.

Marge gulped. "What in the world?"

"Infected! Wererat!" Ella shrieked. She fumbled with the walking stick's buttons. The light began blinking on and off. Which one released the knife? She couldn't remember.

Tomcat hissed and leapt for the rat just as it launched itself at Marge, and Ella gave up on trying to free the hidden knife and instead walloped the cane against the spot the rat had been a second before.

Marge screamed and fell onto her back, tripping over the corpse of the tinker as the snarling rat ran up her skirt. Tomcat darted in as the rat clawed at her face, but he was caught by a stray kick as Marge struggled, shrieking and flailing, and he was sent flying into the side of the tinker's canvas tent, which then collapsed on top of him.

The mule bawled as Ella swatted at the rat. Unable to get a clear shot, she accidentally whacked Marge on the head. Behind them, the bushes rustled, and a giant black wolf burst through. The wolf bound over Ella and landed on Marge, pinning her down, and its jaws snapped onto the rat's spine and flung it away into the shadows with a flick of its powerful head.

Ella trod on a stray ladle, lost her footing and crashed to the ground.

"Help me!" Marge shrieked as the wolf released her, and after scrambling to her knees, clawed her way up the nearest fir tree, leaving Ella to face the gigantic wolf alone.

Heart in her throat, Ella gripped the walking stick, ready to defend herself, when the black wolf turned its head to reveal a streak of white fur over its right eye.

"Wulf?" Ella blinked as the panting creature caught her eye and nodded. It leaned in and licked the back of her hands, and then it was gone.

Relief turned Ella's bones to a momentary pool of jelly until her thoughts caught up with her again, and she called out for Tom. "Tom? Are you hurt?"

The canvas writhed and a white furry face peeped out from the tangle of the tent. "I'm okay," he said, rubbing his forehead where Marge's boot had struck him. "You?"

Ella let out a long sigh and nodded. "Wulf saved us."

"A wolf?" Tomcat said, sounding confused as Ella got to her feet.

She winced as pain flared in a sprained ankle, and she limped over to where the mule, by some miracle of fate was still tethered to the tree, and gently ran her hands over the shaking creature's back.

Ella called out to the midwife, "Marge, did the rat bite you? Come down, let me see."

From the nearby fir tree, the branches shook and a dusting of snow rained down on the remains of the tinker's camp. "I am never setting foot on the ground again!" came an indignant voice.

"If wishes were fishes," Ella muttered to herself. She scooped up a red and orange striped saddle blanket from beside the fire pit, shook out the ice and draped the blanket over the back of the mule, and then, picking up Tomcat, settled him between the mule's shoulder blades. "I'm taking the mule."

"You're not leaving me!" came a dismayed wail.

"Make sure you dress any cuts that wererat gave you with a salve of garlic and colloidal silver."

"I'm not stupid," came a sulky reply from up in the trees.

Ella untied the mule and tugged his lead. "When you get back to Charmington, tell the guards to come and bury this poor, brave man—his sacrifice might have saved the town."

CHAPTER 25

HOME SWEET HOME

ELLA'S HOME, RIVERSIDE COTTAGE, WYLD ENCHANTMENT WOODS.

"So what you're telling me," Tomcat voiced from his perch on the back of Mr Potts' mule, "is that the man called Wulf, who you spoke to in the Huntsman tavern, and who told you he works for Prince John, is actually a werewolf?"

"That's correct," Ella replied, readjusting her grip on the mule's rope harness. With the impediment of her sprained ankle, the remainder of the journey home had been arduously slow, although not as uncomfortable as it might have been, what with the mule to balance against and the backup of her walking stick, but she was extremely relieved when they reached the silver oak and turned off the main path and ventured down to the frozen river in which her home, Riverside Cottage, lay nestled on its own wee island.

A thin band of white smoke wrinkled against the blue sky, rising from the kitchen chimney, suggested the stove hadn't gone out and which itself was a very welcome sight. She wanted nothing more than to sit beside a warm fire in the safety of her own home far from the madness of the day's events and not think about murder or were-infected rats.

Clicking her tongue, and with a swift tug on the lead, Ella was further grateful when the mule stepped out onto the frozen river with little coaxing. No doubt, he had proved a reliable beast for Mr Potts for many years. Ella pushed the twinge of regret aside. There was nothing she could do for Mr Potts. Perhaps she might be able to find out where the travelling salesman was from and write to let his family know what had become of him...

"Look, it's Robinne," Tomcat voiced, interrupting Ella's thoughts and jumping down from the mule when they reached the cottage island embankment. Robinne waved to them from where she stood in front of the barn, a horse brush in one hand, Ella's miniature donkey, Tinkerbelle, beside her.

"I hope you don't mind," Robinne called, continuing her task of brushing the little grey donkey, and gestured to the backyard where

Ella saw the lass must have spent an industrious morning. The chickens were scratching around, the hole in their fence mended, a pile of chopped kindling was stacked neatly beside the back door, and Ella's washing was hung out on the line, the white sheets fluttering in the breeze. "I came to collect some apples for cider making. I thought you would accept a trade of labour for apples."

Ella nodded. "Yes, thank you, my dear." She winced and motioned for Robinne to come and take the mule's rope lead from her as Tomcat disappeared into the pumpkin patch to check on the ripening state of his pumpkin. The plants rippled around him, swaying and bobbing like an affectionate puppy greeting its favourite person.

"Isn't this the travelling tinker's mule?" Robinne frowned, concern suddenly etched across her pretty heart-shaped face while Ella hobbled to the porch steps and unlaced her boot and stripped off her knitted sock. Robinne led the mule into the barn alongside Ella's donkey, and once the two creatures were secured and munching on hay and apples in companionable silence, she inspected Ella's foot, turning it this way and that. "A slight sprain. Should be right in a couple of days if you rest it. I have some clove balm that will help quicken the healing."

Ella smiled. In the past, she and Robinne had had their differences but recently the young woman put aside her distrust of Ella and become a firm ally and valued neighbour.

"What happened?" Robinne asked when suddenly the chickens squawked and ran about the yard in an eruption of feathers. Robinne was on her feet in an instant, grabbing Ella's walking stick. She looked left and right as if seeking to reassure herself that Tom was safely hidden before calling out, "Who's there? Come out before I make you!"

A hand was cautiously raised in the air from behind the chicken coop. "It's Wulf. I am unarmed."

Robinne, scowling darkly, sprinted straight at the coop, stick raised like a weapon, before Ella could call her off. A second later, the lass skidded to a halt and baulked at whatever she saw behind the coop.

"Told you," came Wulf's reply.

Robinne shook her head in apparent disgust, grabbed up the mule's red and orange striped saddle blanket that she had draped over the stable door, and hurled it behind the coop. "Cover yourself up, and come out into the open," she ordered briskly, not lowering the walking stick, still held aloft like a bat.

Wulf, apparently naked beneath the saddle blanket clutched awkwardly about his waist, limped barefoot into the backyard. Despite one eye blackened and swollen shut, a couple of his toes bent at angles to suggest they must be broken, and the way he held his right arm that bore the silver manacle at a funny angle, he bowed gallantly before Ella as if they were meeting in much grander circumstances. "Good day, my lady. I trust you are well."

"You know who this pathetic chicken thief is?" Robinne demanded, prodding the stick into Wulf's shoulder, which caused him to flinch and drop to one knee.

"Mind the shoulder, if you please!" he growled. "Lady Ella can vouch for me."

Ella clutched the porch railing for support and hauled herself upright. "He works for Prince John."

"That's not the sort of recommendation to win you any friends around here," Robinne countered, "and besides, I *know* who you are."

Wulf cocked an ear—a very normal human-shaped ear—and cast a mockingly handsome smile over his injured shoulder at his pretty captor. "As I know you, Robinne, aka the Red Unicorn. I could have caught you last month at the archery contest. Easily. I let you go. That makes us even, no?"

Robinne's determined scowl cracked, surprise softened her features, and for a moment, she was just a young woman without the weight of a brewing rebellion on her shoulders.

If Ella had been in a better mood, she might have said, 'Get a *room*, you two!' But the pain in her aching bones and the tragedy of the past few days had soured her feelings. "I know who *you say* you are, Mr Wulf, but it's Robinne's word I'll take over yours. You understand."

"He's a smuggler," Robinne answered promptly between clenched teeth. "Used to deal with Rum about ten years ago. I was a child, but I remember. You can't trust him."

Wulf sighed. Looked down at his broken toes and then looked up at Ella, his dark eyes acknowledging the painful truth of Robinne's words. "Indeed, she speaks the truth." He shook his head, handsome features full of regret. "I am all those things and worse. My father is..."

His words failed him for a second, but then he drew a breath and held his head high. "My father *was* Arthur, and though he would condemn me himself, but so help me, I swear when I find the man that killed my father, I will rip them limb from limb with my teeth."

CHAPTER 26

WULF'S TALE

"You're Arthur's son!" Tomcat cried, padding up to the odd little gathering in the backyard, his long bushy tail flicking. "But Arthur was told that you were dead!"

Wulf did a double-take at the cat emerging from the pumpkin patch, the snow-dusted vines swaying and twining about him. "Am I the only one hearing the cat talk?" He probed his swollen black eye and mumbled something about having hit his head harder than he thought.

"I think everyone had better come inside," Ella said with a sigh. When would Tom ever learn to hold his tongue? He was nearly as bad as Marge!

Robinne's dismay was also apparent, and she snapped, "Let him in? You can't trust him! I told you he's a smuggler and a thief."

Ella opened the back door into her kitchen. "I'm not saying I trust him, but I'd rather hear his tale in comfort and warmth than out here in the cold. My foot has gone completely numb."

Wulf smirked and cast Robinne a wink, who glared back at him and raised the stick as if she might whack him.

A FEW MINUTES LATER, THEY were all settled in around the scrubbed pine table and enjoying a freshly brewed cup of honey-bark tea as they relaxed in the warmth and familiar comfort of Ella's cottage kitchen.

At Ella's insistence, Robinne assessed and then tended to Wulf's injuries, grumbling as she did so. "How did you do this damage?" Ella asked after Robinne deftly probed Wulf's shoulder to ensure the collarbone wasn't broken.

"I fell into a bear trap," Wulf said, biting back curses and clutching the blanket wrapped about his waist while Robinne moved onto the task of straightening his broken toes. "Sweet mercy, woman! How about a glass of whiskey for my pain?" He swallowed hard when she ignored him and, after a few minutes, gasped, "I followed the scent of the wererat back to a series of nearby caves—I used them myself for smuggling, back in the day, I might add, but the bear trap was new." He continued as if that were the least of the problems. "The rat had escaped from a cage."

"What?" Ella cried aghast. "You mean someone had *kept* a were-infected rat? Why?"

"Tell us first how come you were reported to have died in prison," Tomcat interrupted, "and tell us about this prison tattoo." Robinne followed Tomcat's pawing gesture at Wulf's hand and grabbed it herself to examine the three dots.

Wulf snatched his hand back from Robinne's grasp and ran it self-consciously through his thick black hair. The motion showed off well-defined chest muscles. "They are one and the same. I was offered a choice: take the bite and work for John in secret, and my sentence would be commuted."

"What do you mean, take the bite?"

Wulf indicated the wolf bite scar across his knuckles and Robinne flinched as if putting two and two together.

"Told you," Tomcat voiced smugly to Ella. "Told you Prince John has a secret police force."

"Not so secret if even a cat knows about it," Wulf muttered under his breath.

"But why would John use *criminals*?" Robinne placed heavy emphasis on the word, and folded her arms as if to say to Ella, *And I told you he was no good.*

Wulf shrugged his uninjured shoulder and looked away. Ella narrowed her eyes. Clearly, the lad knew why, but he wasn't about to give away all his master's secrets. "Whatever his reasons, John does trust him," Ella offered. "We all saw Wulf at the archery contest last month standing bodyguard."

Her thoughts drifted to Wulf's father, Arthur, who once had been her own bodyguard. There had been no one she had trusted more.

"I catch people John wants caught. It's what I do." Wulf grinned as if to remind them that, thanks to him, Robinne had remained free.

"Maybe *last* month you worked for the prince," Robinne said tightly. "A lot of things can happen in a month."

Wulf dismissed her implication. "If you won't take my word, take John's. I'm here on his orders."

"Doing what exactly?" Tom spoke up. "You told Ella you were after an escaped prisoner. Who?"

A horrible suspicion seeded in Ella's mind. A finger of fear crawled down her spine. "Magic preserve me! Did Mrs Haversham escape from prison?"

"Mrs Haversham is still alive?" Tomcat meowed, clearly appalled and looking to Ella for answers.

"Not Haversham, though I know who you mean. All the other prisoners fear her..." Wulf shook his head as if to clear it. "No, I'm after a conman. Goes by the name of Van Helsing. He stirs up unfounded fears and then demands large sums of money to provide a false remedy."

Ella hummed to herself. That made sense. It was, however, very neat and tidy. Too neat? Willow had claimed that Van Helsing also worked in the prison as an informer. Maybe Van Helsing had learned something extremely valuable or dangerous, maybe even about John?

"Why does your prince care so much to recapture one lowly conman?" Ella leaned in close. "Reports are that dozens escaped from the Nottingham prison. What makes Van Helsing so special?"

CHAPTER 27

AN UNEXPECTED GUEST

Wulf broke eye contact again, just for a second. "It is not my place to betray my master, suffice to say Van Helsing made a fool of and then stole from John."

"That's very convenient," Robinne replied with a distrustful scowl.

"Now, now," Ella tutted, "we have no reason *not* to trust Wulf..."

Examining Wulf's face, she could see familiarity there. Arthur had worn that earnest look when trying to convince her of something or other many times in the past. How had she not seen the family resemblance before?

"And you have my deepest condolences on the loss of your father. He was a dear friend of mine."

"What?" Robinne straightened. "Arthur is dead? What happened?"

Ella briefly explained, and Wulf lowered his gaze, unable to meet anyone's eye. No doubt, the pain was very fresh and doubly tragic. To think Arthur's boy was not only alive but actually in their town the same night when Arthur had been telling her and Tom of his son's supposed death.

"The last time I saw my father, he made it clear he never wanted to see me again." Wulf idly played with a cup on the tabletop. "Hansel tried to convince me last night," he said softly, "to go talk to him, reveal myself." He half-shrugged and rubbed his fingers over the bite scar on his right hand. "I would have none of it, I was too proud... If only I had listened to him."

Tomcat's whiskers fanned. "Hansel..." He shared a look with Ella.

Ella reached out and placed her hands on top of Wulf's. He flinched but didn't remove his hands. A look of hurt and regret in his eyes made him seem a lot younger than the years and deeds of his varied life had etched upon him. "Tom and I ran into Hansel last night."

"That's right!" Tomcat's whiskers shivered. "Gretel was telling him not to go to see Arthur, to 'stay out of it!'"

"You think he went anyway?" Hope sparked in Wulf's dark eyes. "Maybe Hansel told Arthur I was alive despite my wishes...?"

Ella nodded. "I am sure of it. I feel it in my bones." She squeezed Wulf's hands.

Wulf suddenly cocked his head. "Footsteps," he murmured, on his feet in one smooth motion, and he grabbed a large bread knife, just as a crisp *rat-tat-tat* echoed on the front door and a female voice sang out, "Good mother Ella, are you home?"

Tomcat sprinted out of the kitchen and down the passage to investigate, but Ella had already recognised the voice. It was Miss Hillary Harper. The girl from the post office. What could she possibly want?

Ella looked up to see Robinne's eyes drift across Wulf's bare torso in an assessing glance of admiration.

Of course, attraction was the motivation. Hillary's conversation that morning had implied the girl had a fancy for young Tom, and considering how persistent Harold had been in his unwelcome attentions, why should the daughter be any different?

"Quick, hide upstairs," Ella ordered the confused youngsters in her kitchen as Tom trotted back. "People think Tom is unconscious and recovering in my cottage, I think Hillary is here for proof—you too, Tom, upstairs."

"Why me?" Tomcat muttered, crossing his arms.

"Very cat-like," Ella whispered ironically, mimicking Tom's pose, and with a defeated sigh, he bounded up the stairs after the other two with no further protests.

After shooing everyone away to hide, Ella called out to Hillary at the front door, "Just lift the latch, dear. I'm in the back."

The young post office woman let herself in and bustled into the kitchen, her big wide eyes darting here and there. Her expression betrayed both hesitation and unbridled curiosity. Who knows what gory stories Harold might have told her? It spoke volumes of her attachment for Tom that she would brave the forest and the townsfolk's gossip!

It occurred to Ella that if she played her cards right, she could find out if Hillary had access to the records room, and maybe even have the lass aid her investigation into whoever had tried to purchase Arthur's business. That would be extremely useful.

"Good mother Ella, whatever happened to you?" Hillary said, eyeing Ella's bare ankle propped up on a stool. The lass untied the strings of her plain brown cloak and draped it over a chair and then placed a bundle of papers she had been carrying onto the table.

"Just a sprain, do not concern yourself." Ella gestured to the kettle. "I apologise for not getting up. Do help yourself to a cup of honey-bark tea. What goodies do you have there?"

"A couple of letters for Tom came in on the barge recently..." Her eyes never met Ella's but constantly scanned the room. "And I bought a copy of today's newspaper. I know Tom likes doing the crossword. Where is he?"

Ella cast her gaze up towards the loft, relieved that the muffled noises had ceased. "I'm afraid he is very unwell—unconscious."

"I can read to him," Hillary said eagerly, scooping up the letters addressed to Tom. "It's supposed to help, you know."

"Is it?" Ella said when a loud thump echoed above. She cursed her luck. What were they *doing* up there? "Never mind that. Probably the wind banging a shutter."

But Hillary was already climbing the stairs to the loft. "What if he fell out of bed?"

"I'm not sure that's appropriate for a young lady to enter a gentleman's bedroom!" Ella voiced helplessly in warning. Her joints stiff from the long walk, she struggled to get to her feet and chase after the post office girl.

On reaching her loft bedroom, Ella bumped into Hillary, who was standing stock still just inside the doorway. Ella's heart sang in relief at the normality of the scene presented before her. Robinne was perched on the window seat, reading a copy of *Cinderella*. Wulf was tucked up in Ella's feather bed, his back to the room, the bedclothes drawn up over his head. And Tomcat was curled on the foot of the brass bed frame.

"Anything I can help you with?" Robinne enquired with a bored yawn.

Hillary, brow pinched, her hands curled into tight fists, crushing the letters. "Fine. I see. That's the way it is, is it?" She pushed past Ella and stomped back down the steps, muttering under her breath, "I'll see myself out. Good day."

Without looking back, she flung the scrunched letters onto the kitchen table, gathered up her cloak and stormed off.

Ella rolled her eyes, clasped the handrail and called out, "Thank you for bringing the letters, that was very kind!" When she heard the front door slam, she returned to the bedroom.

Tomcat lifted his head, green eyes wide with confusion. "Why was she so upset?"

Ella was about to voice her suspicions of young Hillary's jealous affections when she spied the striped mule blanket folded at the foot of the bed. "Magic preserve, Wulf, please tell me you are decent under there!"

Wulf rolled over, sweeping back Ella's nightcap that he'd covered his dark hair with. "Forgive me, our options were limited." He lowered the cotton sheets to reveal he was also dressed in Ella's best nightgown.

BAD NEWS AND BAD VIEWS

Market Square, Charmington Castle.

"You're doing the right thing," Tomcat voiced at Ella's side as they trekked across the frosty street on their way to Charmington Castle.

"Yes, yes, better safe than sorry," Ella muttered, her stick tapping across the cobbles as she limped onward. Despite the hour, the weariness in her bones and the pain in her ankle, they had returned to Charmington with two important missions. One was to check up on the tenancy deeds surrounding anything to do with Arthur's business. The other more pressing task was to check up on Wulf's story. Was he truly still working for Prince John?

Though she was loath to admit it, and every instinct told her that Wulf was a man of his word, she had been tricked before by people she knew and trusted. Mrs Haversham had poisoned Ella's own dear sister Cinderella. She would be a fool indeed to make such a mistake again! And with that painful suspicion in mind, she had left Robinne to watch over Wulf and crept out of the cottage with Tomcat in tow.

Outside the castle, there were several groups of townsfolk spread across the market square, and more gathering all the time in the twilight. At the base of one of the streetlamps, Marge, standing slightly raised above a knot of people, was drawing a curious crowd of onlookers around her. Ella knew with cold certainty that the midwife used the stolen stockpot as her 'soap box'.

"Look at me!" the midwife wailed, pointing at her badly scratched face. "I spent hours alone in the woods—fighting for my life! Defending myself from an army of wererats!"

Army? Ella tutted. There had been one rat. Terrifying, admittedly, but hardly an army.

Surveying the captivated faces, Ella realised there was one notable exception. Van Helsing. Why wasn't he here? Surely, this was exactly what he wanted? Instil the fear and then claim he was the only one with the remedy. That's what Wulf had said he'd do. But then again, perhaps Van Helsing was still hiding from Sibylla's guards?

"I ask you, is it good enough?" Marge shouted, jabbing a hand up at the castle.

"No!" roared back the citizens, entranced by her outrage.

"We demand better protection!" shouted Mistress Fairweather. "We pay our taxes!"

"And the rents are going up!" Mr Beau the shoeshine man added, gesturing to the spot he favoured beside the public noticeboard.

"Do you pay rent by the square footage or the location?" someone asked him out of apparent curiosity, but before she heard the reply, Ella spied something more serious and she ventured over to the other side of the square where the dilapidated gallows was situated in the far corner.

Several people were lighting torches! Actual torches. The ends were coated in pitch, and a ring had been placed around the gallows where Bron the baker was chained to the bottom step. Willow's one-eared poodle, Mr Puddles, was curled up asleep in the baker's lap.

"Stay back, good mother Ella," one of the torch-lighting men cautioned her. "Werewolves can't control themselves when they turn." He pointed to the horizon where the sun was low in the sky above the snow-covered mountains. The sky was streaked with pink and grey. "Full moon will rise come sunset. Then the werewolf will be revealed."

Ella exchanged glances with Tomcat at her feet. Considering that the only werewolf she knew of was tucked up in her cottage under the watchful eye of Robinne, it made the appearance of a werewolf in town extremely unlikely. After all, what were the chances there were *two* werewolves?

"Where is Chelton?" she asked the baker. "I thought he was looking after you?"

"They made him go fetch a cleaver," Bron began, looking abashed.

"An axe," the torch-lighter interrupted. "We agreed it needed to be an axe. Chop your head off when you turn!"

"I'm not a werewolf," Bron wailed, getting to his feet. "Good mother Ella, please! Can't you convince them?" His motion woke the poodle and Mr Puddles perked up his solitary ear and, spying Tomcat, started barking.

"Back, stay back!" bellowed the citizen. "Bad dog!"

Ella withdrew, sensing that her and Tomcat's presence wasn't going to aid either the baker or Mr Puddles. Only the full moon would reveal their innocence.

She hurried on to the castle as best she could, biting her tongue at the pain in her sprained ankle as she limped down the covered walkway. On days like today, Ella acknowledged there was a disadvantage to living so far from town.

"Why don't you go talk to Sibylla by yourself? I'll go nosey around the town hall," Tomcat voiced as Ella paused at the unobtrusive side door that she favoured using as an entrance into the castle. "And see if I find an open window, or maybe someone working late..."

"I don't think that's a good idea. We should stick together."

"I'm just as capable as you, and we should split the tasks." Tomcat sat on his haunches, his fluffy tail flicking.

"Yes, but you don't know where the records room is, and it's a labyrinth of corridors under the town hall and post office. You can't just ask someone to show you the way," Ella said logically. "Besides, I thought you wanted to visit the summer garden? To see the goldfish?"

He had such a love for animals. It reminded her of her sister Cinderella. She was forever bringing home injured rabbits and squirrels. She practically set up a hospital for them in the stables when she was a little girl. And when she was older, she even managed to convince Mrs Haversham to donate a considerable sum towards establishing a charitable sanctuary to care for the town's animal population. Ella's smile fell away as she was reminded of Mrs Haversham. How was it after all this time, even thinking of the woman set her heart beating in fear? Haversham was safely locked away. Deep within the Nottingham prison. Never to inflict pain on an innocent again.

Tomcat's ears perked up. "Not the fish. I wanted to go look at the turtle. To see if he's actually a turtle or a tortoise—according to *The Guide,* you can tell by their feet."

Ella rolled her eyes. "*The Guide!* If it weren't for that wretched *Guide* and all the nonsense Van Helsing was spouting, all those people wouldn't be out there waving flaming torches!" Ella sighed, and pushed her feelings deep down. Bickering wouldn't solve any of their current problems, and he did have a point. It would be quicker if they split the tasks. "Just be careful!" she relented. "Don't get caught talking, or you'll find yourself strung up with poor Baker Bron and Mr Puddles."

Tomcat saluted, mimed stitching his lips and scampered off. At least having Tom out of the way meant he was less likely to get them both in trouble by talking in front of Sibylla...

Ella closed the stout castle door behind her and breathed a sigh of relief as the solid walls of her former home shut out the noise and accusations hurled around the market square beyond.

In situations like these, it crossed her mind that the comforts and conveniences of returning to live at the castle might outweigh the compromises that also would entail... But always her guilt pricked at her. What if Richard or his child returned? She had to keep the cottage in good order for them. Abandoning the cottage was like admitting they would never return. She wasn't ready to accept that yet.

TENTATIVELY, ELLA SLID OPEN ONE of the twin doors into the castle library and peeped inside. A fire burned merrily in the grand marble fireplace. Her sister Sibylla was nestled in one of the leather armchairs, turning over pages of an old family album.

"Just place it on the side table," Sibylla muttered as if expecting a servant to have delivered something. On realising it wasn't a servant, her scowl deepened at the intrusion, but then, not unkindly, she said, "Sister, you're limping." She was on her feet in a trice, the family album tucked away out of sight on a shelf, and she assisted Ella to the other vacant leather chair. Sibylla took Ella's walking stick and set it to one side.

For a moment, Ella thought her sister might actually kneel down and strip off Ella's boot to attend to the injury herself, but as if suddenly remembering her station, Sibylla backed off and tugged on the velvet bellpull near the mantle. When a servant's head peeked around the door a moment later, Sibylla told them, "Fetch Goldilocks to me, at once."

Sibylla paced back and forth across the lush white floor rug, her purple silk skirts swishing, and Ella braced herself for a scolding about the perils of living alone in the forest. A scolding which didn't come. "We need to talk. About Richard."

"Richard?" Whatever could Sibylla want to discuss about Richard? Could she have found out where he was? Stunned, Ella sat forward when a tap at the door announced Goldilocks' arrival, and she could only bite her tongue once more as the little woman set down her box of hair products and fussed and clucked over Ella's sprained ankle.

Goldilocks unlatched the box, and it opened out into clever expanding compartments filled with all sorts of combs, clips and perfumes. Fossicking around and removing an inner tray, Goldilocks reached much deeper into the box than space should have allowed.

Goldilocks was like Ace, a craftswoman, though she had turned her magical healing talents to hairdressing when magic had been banned in their kingdom. Clearly, though, there were times she still put her magic touch to use. She extracted a slim amber wand from a hidden compartment, and then said aloud, "Hold your breath: one, two, three." Tapped Ella's ankle with the wand, which shimmered, and the pain was gone. "Shall I paint your toes while I'm here?" Goldilocks held up a little bottle filled with a pale pink goop. "You'd look gorgeous in sugar plum pink!"

"Thank you, no." Ella rubbed her ankle. Magic preserve, what a relief. She watched Goldilocks packing away her collection of accessories and toyed with the idea of asking if Goldilocks might also relieve the arthritis in her knees when she caught Sibylla scowling. If she was going to ask a favour, she couldn't waste it on herself. "Sister, I came here tonight because I need to use your magic mirror to talk to Prince John."

"Whatever for?" Sibylla looked suspicious. "You couldn't get away from him fast enough after the archery contest last month."

"I'm trying to track whoever killed Arthur. I need John to confirm some details."

"Arthur's really dead?" Sibylla appeared genuinely shocked. "What was that nonsense about him being a werewolf?"

"Oh, yes," cooed Goldilocks with the familiarity of a trusted servant. "You've been in the rent talks all day. I told them not to disturb you with that news about poor Arthur."

"Did either of you know he was a werewolf?" Sibylla blinked at both of them.

"That's untrue. He wasn't a werewolf," Ella stated. "That's some madness the townsfolk have latched on to. I can only assume because they saw the wolf smash through his window, put two and two together and got five!" Ella took a breath. She wasn't angry at the townsfolk. She was angry at herself. Arthur was her friend, and yet he had been planning on leaving Charmington. Perhaps without telling her... She shook the hurt feelings away. Now was not the time to dwell on her past failings as a friend. Now was the time to solve his murder. "But yes, it's sadly true that he has...passed away."

"How?"

"Katie heard the baker was actually a werewolf, and he ate Arthur all up." Goldilocks darted over to the alcove where a balcony overlooked the market square below and pulled back the curtain. "See, they've got Bron tied up outside. Waiting on the full moon, I suppose."

They all peered down to the square below, where a bright ring of flickering torches illuminated the gallows. Citizens must have seen the light spilling out from the curtain being moved as suddenly people were pointing up and shouting about their taxes.

Sibylla's lips thinned in a grimace that Ella recognised as her sister's last nerve-fraying. Sibylla waved Goldilocks towards the adjoining map room in which was the desk where the magic mirror was set up. "Put the mirror connection through to John's secretary, and see if he's available."

Goldilocks clapped her hands in glee. "Magic, twice in one day!"

Sibylla drew Ella's attention back to her. "After you speak to John, you and I need to talk." She waved a hand at the gathering throngs jumping up and down outside. "I warn you now, this is the least of our troubles."

Ella didn't know what was more alarming. Her sister's revelation there was trouble brewing or that she wanted to include Ella. 'Our' was not a word Sibylla favoured when things were going her way. Something must be gravely wrong indeed.

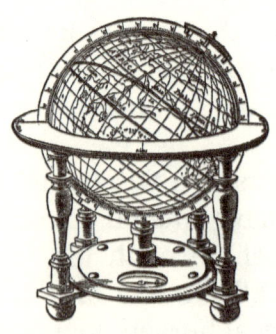

CHAPTER 29

THE TRUTH ABOUT RICHARD

MAP ROOM, CHARMINGTON CASTLE.

Ella peered into a large round mirror about a foot wide, propped up on an ornate, dark oak desk. The last time Ella had seen Sibylla's magic mirror, the glass had been broken, not to mention it was a much smaller handheld version. Clearly, this new desktop mirror was an expensive upgrade. While pondering the lavish expense, Ella's reflection faded, and another person peered back at her. Prince John, regent of the neighbouring kingdom of Sherwood.

The room in which the prince sat was decorated in a similar fashion, although behind him were several old portraits rather than maps, and she wondered if that room was his library or private study. How odd. To be able to see right into people's homes.

John was moving, swaying side to side in his swivel desk chair. The back of his chair repeatedly revealed and then obscured a portrait that caught Ella's eye. Was it meant to be of John? The man was blond like him, but younger, clean-shaven, and far more handsome. Some vanity portrait, no doubt.

"Is it on? I can never...oh yes, I see you there. Lady Ella, what a *charming* pleasure to see you again. No pun intended." The prince smirked.

No pun intended. What a liar, Ella thought, but managed to school her face to mask her repulsion. What was it about John that she found so creepy?

Ella pushed down her unsettled feelings. Now was not the time for her personal dislike of this man to put her off her task. So what if John had a painting done to only show his good side? Vanity was not a crime.

"Your Highness, I beg pardon for intruding upon your evening," she began.

John waved off her concerns and lifted a tall crystal decanter filled with wine or sherry into view. "Not at all, not at all. In fact, you join me in a little private celebration. I received some very good news today." He poured the wine into a golden goblet. "Anyway, tell me how I can help. Your wish is my command," he added with a wink and chuckle.

Ugh. Genie jokes.

"Are you able to confirm that Wulf is still in your employment?" Ella steepled her fingers together, trying to get a better look at the portrait, but John's tall wingback chair blocked her view.

John's head lurched up, and he plonked the decanter down. "Oh lord, what's he done now? Bitten some pretty young thing? I swear I'll have to get him fixed! Haha."

"But he *does* work for you?"

"Yes, yes, absolutely. Provided the silver manacle is still on." John unconsciously rubbed his wrist. "Er, does he happen to have the silver manacle?"

Ella's eyes narrowed. She had thought there was something odd about that piece of jewellery. Was John implying that Wulf was magically bound to him in some way? Maybe she should change tack. "Let's cut to the chase. What exactly is Wulf doing here on your orders?"

John looked cagey. "I suppose you've mentioned this to Queen Sibs?"

"Currently, I haven't informed my queen." Ella tried to glower and look like she was indignant. "Unless you give me a reason to."

John relaxed, sat back and picked up his wine. Held it aloft. "I like your style, Lady E, no nonsense. So, here's the goss. We had something of a prison breakout recently. But good old Wulf has rounded up the blighters. Only a few strays—" He grinned as if pleased to have inserted another awful dog joke. "I told Wulfie boy not to create a fuss, and I promise you I'll give him a hit on the nose with a rolled-up newspaper if he causes any more bother on your side of the border. How's that?"

"Exactly who is he after?" Ella steepled her fingers again. "How many and what sort of danger do they represent? Is there one called Rooster among them?"

John set the drink down and opened a drawer on his desk. "I can show you the list right here." He flashed a reward notice in front of the mirror. A poster for Van Helsing. "Just this last chap." The prince examined the poster, his lips pushed out in a facial shrug. "Not dangerous according to his deets." John made eye contact, expression earnest. "This Van Helsing chap is a thief. Stole some valuables from me after I was very kind to him."

"What items?"

John sat back and spread his hands. "Same old, same old, you know what thieves are like, anything that sparkles. Let's see if the old brainbox can recall. I'm sure Wulfie mentioned something about a box of treasure..."

Looking away, the prince leaned back in his chair, hands folded up onto his head as if thinking. Ella took the opportunity to scrutinise the portrait behind him. That's when it struck her. The portrait wasn't of John, it wasn't trying to capture his good side, to distil his features into their best, most handsome form. It was a stylised portrait of another man entirely.

A man Ella knew. A man she had been in love with. Richard.

But no, *her* Richard had a beard all the time she had known him. The man in this portrait was clean-shaven. No, she must be mistaken. It couldn't be. It just couldn't be. Richard was a kind, loyal man. He was a woodcutter. Not a prince play-acting at being a commoner.

"Who is that man?" Ella asked and John glanced over his shoulder and smiled.

"Oh, yes, that's my fabled big bro, Richard. You and I were chatting about his exploits when we met at the archery contest, you recall."

"The one who disappeared?" she replied to John, trying to suppress the roiling sick feeling that was building in her stomach. Dreading that her face must be giving her away.

"That's right," John added, stroking his chin, "still, shouldn't complain. If it weren't for old Richie running off, I'd just be the spare and not the heir."

Ella swallowed. Her worst fears were confirmed. But how? How could it be, and why would Richard deceive them—*her*?

John sat forward and grinned broadly. "And in a few months, old Richie is going to be officially declared dead, and that means I'll be made king proper and not have to suffer this regent title nonsense." John held up his glass of wine and saluted the portrait. "It's the reason for my wee indulgence today."

"Congratulations," Ella managed, feeling that some response was called for.

"I don't want to jinx it..." He grabbed a pen from a golden desk set and licked the nib. "But shall I add you and Sibs to the coronation guest list?"

"I would be honoured," Ella replied, drawing upon all her years of stoicism to utter those words with a cool demeanour while inside her brain was screaming at her, *Richard was a fraud! Richard was a liar! He tricked you!*

"Thank you for your time, Your Highness." Ella waved Goldilocks to come forward and assist with disconnecting the mirror—her brain in such turmoil she couldn't for the life of her remember how it was done.

"My pleasure, Lady E, my pleasure," John said gallantly, likewise signalling for assistance on his side of the mirror. He waved and said, "Toodle pip, cheerio," before his image cut out, and Ella was left staring at her own gaunt reflection.

CHAPTER 30

BUT WAIT, THERE'S MORE BAD NEWS

LIBRARY, CHARMINGTON CASTLE.

"How long have you known?"

At her sister's question, Sibylla turned from staring into the fire burning in the library grate. She gestured to the side table between the leather armchairs and the glasses of sherry laid out and awaiting Ella's return from the map room.

Ella collapsed onto the other leather chair and set a glass of sherry to her lips. The sweet burn made her throat hum, and she set it aside. Her thoughts were already tangled into knots. Oblivion wasn't the refuge she sought. She wanted answers.

"You saw Richard's portrait, then?" Sibylla muttered, drumming her fingers on the dark leather, her brightly painted fingernails glinting in the firelight like small knives. Sibylla ceased drumming and folded her hands neatly on her lap and sighed. "I found out who he really was not long after Cinders passed away."

"What?" Ella blurted, rising from her seat. "But that was years—decades—ago! Why didn't you tell me?"

Sibylla held up her palms. "Though you may not believe me, in part I did it to protect you."

"Me? But how would *not knowing* the truth protect me—and why do you even think I needed protection?" Ella scolded, folding her arms tightly across her thin body.

Sibylla shook her head. "Sister, Sister. Look at yourself. Richard had you wrapped around his finger from day one—"

"Oh! That's nonsense!" Ella turned away, picked up the fire poker and stirred up the embers.

"I saw how he made you act. You lost your wand for misuse of wishes—wishes that aided Richard. You never would have behaved that way without his influence. He used you." Sibylla rose to her feet and, to Ella's surprise, placed a gentle hand on her shoulder. "I had to make the hard decisions, so that's what I did."

Used me.

Never in her darkest hour had Ella let such a thought enter her mind, but she thought it now. Let it wash over her like grief.

Ella swallowed her tears, brushed off the kind gesture and flung herself back into the armchair. After gulping down the burning sherry, she said, "So, he lied to us. Do you know why? I just can't understand it. What could he have thought his deception would gain him? Prince or woodcutter, his station made no difference to Cinderella. She still had to give up her magic in order to marry."

Sibylla's expression remained remarkably neutral. "I cannot say." She gestured to the glass door of the adjoining map room. "But Wyld Kingdom has resisted pressure from Sherwood encroaching upon our lands for centuries. We have always been the wyld beating heart of magic, while they are just the spill over, the dregs."

"A claim for land?" Ella sat forward as she ran the idea over in her mind. "Their child..."

Sibylla nodded grimly. "Indeed. Heir to the Sherwood throne half born of Wyld kingdom."

"He could claim the title over the two kingdoms!" Ella was aghast. "Merge us into one!"

Sibylla nodded. "You understand our predicament. Our land is small. Magic made us powerful, but our rules of inheritance held the peace. Made us less desirable to conquer because we never sought power beyond our boundary."

Another thought occurred. And despite the confused feelings of loss and betrayal, Ella's heart beat hard as she asked, "Is Richard dead? What happened to him and his child?"

Sibylla leaned against the mantle, her stony demeanour crumbling in a gesture that revealed weariness. "I have been trying to find that out for nearly as long as I have known the truth." Her shoulders drooped. "Every trail has turned cold. Every clue faded to nothing." She looked up and met her sister's eye, her expression both a mixture of resolve and pity. "I simply do not know."

Ella swallowed. Though logic said that, surely, they must be dead, the foolish stubborn part of her, the part that had always yearned for Richard despite knowing he would never be hers, simply couldn't let him go. "Hope is the cruellest emotion of all..." she murmured, and her sister nodded.

In the shared silence, there came raised voices from outside, and Ella glanced at the balcony windows. Had the full moon arisen? What was going on out there?

As if sensing Ella was about to go and take a look, Sibylla added, "Ella, there is something else you need to know. More bad news. Worse than Richard."

"Worse than Richard being a liar? Magic preserve me, will this day never end?"

Sibylla paced the white fur rug as if not quite sure where to begin. At last, she stopped pacing, smoothed her skirts and said, "The kingdom is in financial ruins."

"What?" shouted Ella, launching herself to her feet. "How is this possible? How did *you* let this happen?"

"Me?" refuted Sibylla, her voice filled with outrage. "Without *me*, this would have happened years ago. And not because of me—but you! We are at the cusp right now. For years, our reserves have been declining. Our whole economy was based on magic—the schools, the spas, the products! No magic means no income!"

"Why is that my fault?" Ella folded her arms. "How dare you! You're the one who banned magic! So un-ban it!"

"I only enforced what was the will of the people. The population turned against magic because of Haversham, because of Cinderella and because of you—yes, you, though you're too proud to admit it. Now just shut up and listen because you will hear this!"

Ella gulped. Stunned into silence.

"Prince John is ambitious. Don't let his merry-jester act trick you as you fell for Richard's snake-oil charms. I need you to back me, to support me as both your sister and your queen."

Ella stood back as if her sister's words had slapped her. "Are you accusing me of *disloyalty*?"

"Yes, I am. And it stops today. Whatever you and John are plotting. You need to get over yourself, suck up your pride and do what is right for our kingdom."

Ella didn't know where to look. This onslaught was extremely unfair. When had she ever acted against the best interests of Wyld Enchantment Woods? She had devoted her life to the kingdom and its people.

A thought occurred. A dreadful thought.

Could it be that somehow Sibylla thought she had actually known that Richard was the heir to Sherwood? That they had been working together to overthrow Sibylla? It all suddenly made a terrible kind of sense. "Magic preserve, you thought I knew—didn't you? You thought I knew that Richard was a prince. All this time?"

CHAPTER 31

WEREWOLVES AND WEREBEARS, OH MY!

Sibylla nodded. "Yes."

"I don't know what to say…" Ella mumbled.

Sibylla suddenly grabbed Ella by the shoulders. "Swear it, swear to me on the keys to the kingdom that you didn't know who Richard truly was!"

Ella swallowed. Stunned by the desperation in her sister's voice. The keys to the kingdom? That was a strong oath. Did Sibylla truly believe Ella would betray their kingdom? "I swear by the keys. I did not know! My first loyalty is always to Charmington. Tell me what I must do to help you fix this mess, and I will do it. You have my word."

Sibylla appeared placated. Her demeanour relaxed, she released Ella and turned away. "That's good to hear, because I'm going to have to increase the rents threefold, and someone is going to have to convince the citizens to swallow that pill without rioting."

"Threefold!" Ella burst out. "Is there no other way?"

"I am working on it, trust me." Sibylla shook her head wearily and poured them both another sherry. "So far, I have come up with selling assets, land, or renting out my home for wedding parties. There's an idea. How about you find a rich husband?"

"After you," Ella returned the joke. Indeed, it was no laughing matter, but what else could they do? "Worse comes to worst, I suppose we could ask Merlin for help."

Sibylla cocked her head. "Ugh. And have the place overrun by the pompous Pendragons and their smug band of knights?"

Her sister had a point. Ella sighed. "Do you suspect that John knows Richard married our sister Cinderella, or that they had a child?"

"He knows something, but I can hardly have *him* reveal what he knows without giving away what *I* know."

"I see your predicament. But I have news. Just now, John said that Richard will officially be declared dead shortly, and then *he* will be crowned king. Once that happens, surely whatever claim Richard's child could have on any inheritance from either side must be overruled."

"Unless John inherits any titles or property that should have gone to Richard?"

"Magic preserve..."

Both sisters sat back, contemplating what such repercussions might be, when into the strained truce born of a shared concern for their country, voices from the square intruded upon the inner sanctum of the library in a chant of, "Off with his head! Off with his head!"

"Now what?" Sibylla voiced in annoyance at the chanting. She drew back the thick velvet balcony curtain a crack, and they both peered out to see townsfolk surrounding the gallows. Chelton the butcher was waving one of the flaming torches, fending off a crowd who were yelling and pointing while Bron cowered on the steps. There was no sign of Mr Puddles.

Oh dear, what had become of Willow's troublesome dog now?

Ella glanced up at the full moon shining down on everyone. Clearly, doing nothing to allay the people's fears. "Setting the financial worries aside, you need to put a stop to this nonsense."

"You mean it's more than just the rental increase that has stirred them up?" Sibylla murmured as if having misunderstood the situation. "Where are the town guards? Axel should be stamping this out."

Ella wondered if, in all her worries over the financial crisis, her sister had forgotten that Axel was serving time in their lockup as punishment for gross misconduct. If she brought it up would Sibylla simply have him released to bring the situation under control? But come to think of it, where was Cassidy and the other night watch? Surely, this fell under her jurisdiction?

Sibylla wrenched open the balcony door and strode out, the frosty air swirling about her. "Silence!" Sibylla roared down at her people and stamped her foot. "What is the meaning of this insubordination?"

Awkward silence washed over the crowds. A brief muttering and fidgeting followed until, finally, Marge stepped forward. She brandished a shiny new ladle at the butcher and baker. "They are infected! A werebear and a werewolf! It *shouldn't* be allowed!"

"What?" Sibylla drawled incredulously. "Has everyone gone completely insane?"

Ella joined her sister at the railing and gestured to the full moon illuminating the square. "What about your test?" she shouted down, her breath puffing out a cloud of steam in the night air. "According to *The Guide*, a werebeast is revealed by the moon!"

"But, but, but," one of the other people stuttered, pointing at Chelton. "He's the size of a bear!"

"He's as hairy as a bear!" cried a second.

"Therefore, he's clearly a bear. You can't argue with science!"

"Werebear! Werebear!" The chant sprang up, led by Marge banging a ladle against her ill-gotten stockpot.

Sibylla and Ella exchanged glances. First rule of governing was *You can't reason with a mob.*

"Idiots," growled Sibylla under her breath. She stomped back into the library and slammed the balcony door shut behind them and then turned to Ella. "Tell me, how did Arthur die?"

"I've been asking myself the same question," Ella replied, grateful to resume her toasty spot beside the fire. "It appears to have been a random dog attack, but..."

"Somehow, the townsfolk have jumped to the conclusion it was actually a *werewolf*? Are they mad?" Sibylla cast a shrewd glance towards the balcony as if weighing up the pros and cons of this distraction keeping them from dwelling on the rental increases.

"Unfortunately, there was a rather perfectly timed wolf attack in broad daylight, and Van Helsing drove off the wolf by playing his flute."

Even as Ella said the words aloud, a little inner voice pointed out, it *was* perfectly timed.

It certainly looked like Wulf was stopped by the pipe. But can you trust what you saw? Knowing that Arthur, who disowned his own child, is dead? What if Van Helsing and Wulf were a team? One wants money, and one...revenge? Arthur was killed by a bite, and how many werewolves are there currently on the loose?

"Van Helsing?" Sibylla gagged as if recalling her earlier encounter outside the town hall. "That revolting man wearing a string of rodent skulls?"

"He calls himself a supernatural exterminator. I can't vouch for that. But he did steal valuables from John."

Sibylla's eyes narrowed, and she looked interested. "Do you think John would *pay* to have the man captured and the items safely returned?"

"I can find out..." Assuming that Wulf could be trusted to tell her... could it be that Wulf wanted whatever Van Helsing had stolen for himself? What could it be? A box of sparkly treasure, John had said, but Ella doubted the vagueness. If something specific had been stolen from John, he'd know exactly what. Perhaps the key to the silver manacle? The key to Wulf's freedom?

Chapter 32

Ella and Tom Make Plans

"Do that," Sibylla instructed Ella, smoothly falling into her role as queen and commander, "and I'll tell our citizens out there that I'll pay whatever fee this exterminator wants. That will keep them quiet and it will lure him in. You will negotiate with him, naturally. I can't be seen to deal with such people. News of that would draw every fortune hunter from Avalon to Timbuktu."

Ella wanted to refuse, to remind Sibylla that she was her sister, not her personal assistant. But she had just agreed to do what her sister asked to benefit their kingdom. And another part of her pointed out that this gave her a legitimate reason for questioning Van Helsing. First and foremost, she wanted to find out *why* Arthur had been killed and by whom. If Wulf's grief over the death of his father was an act, then Van Helsing might know.

"Very good, Your Highness," Ella said, bowing and clicking her heels. "At once, Your Majesty."

Sibylla rolled her eyes. "That wasn't funny when we were children, and it's not funny now."

"As you say, Your Grandness." Bow. Curtsey. "Shall I fluff your pillows before I leave?" Touch of the forelock. Slowly backing out of the room. "Goodnight, Exalted One, may flights of angels—"

"Oh, just leave—watch the table! Act your age for once."

Ella was surprised to find she was actually smiling on leaving her sister's presence for perhaps the first time in many years.

ELLA WAS CONCERNED THAT TOMCAT might have gotten himself into trouble nosing around the town hall and wouldn't be waiting in the summer garden, so she let out a breath on seeing him there.

Tomcat was stretched out on his tummy, paws under his chin, kicking his legs back and gazing into the summer garden's pond.

Seemingly mesmerised by the inhabitants lazily sculling through the floating lilies and warm waters.

Perhaps she should give him more freedom. He was a grown man, after all, not a child and not her cat.

"I'm sorry I took so long," Ella began, standing next to him and observing the orange goldfish swimming gracefully alongside the turtle. She regarded the large creature. Was the pond big enough for him? He looked happy, but how could she really tell? Was this a turtle's idea of paradise? Or was he aware he was a captive? Just another decorative bauble in Sibylla's collection? Ella shook off her strange thoughts. "Did you find your answer? Tortoise or turtle?"

"Turtle!" Tomcat said, gathering his legs under himself and sitting upright. "What about you?"

"Wulf spoke the truth. He still works for John. Van Helsing is wanted for the theft of something valuable from John himself. He wouldn't say what, he was quite cagey about it..."

Tomcat's ears twitched and dipped. "Whatever could it be?" They both contemplated the possibilities for a second. "Probably not the sheepskin suit! But maybe the rat skull necklace? Or the flute?"

Ella nodded to herself as she stared into the pond, her own reflection distorted in the ripples as the turtle breached the surface. "The flute indeed..." She thought back on how the black wolf—how Wulf had smashed through the glass window to try to reach Van Helsing. Was that an act of pure impulse? Of desperation? Or a planned and calculated event? "I was thinking perhaps that Wulf might have a vested interest in whatever Van Helsing is harbouring."

Tomcat sat up and tilted his head left and right. "Go on."

"What does any prisoner crave?"

"Their freedom!" Tomcat stood up on his hind legs, blinking green eyes. "Both Van Helsing and Wulf were prisoners in Nottingham... But Wulf isn't a prisoner anymore."

Ella shook her head. "Technically, but he's not *entirely* free. He traded time in prison to work for John."

"And you think maybe Van Helsing did the same, but somehow he broke free of the deal?"

Ella shrugged. "That's an interesting idea. Mostly, I was thinking that whatever Van Helsing stole might be the key to Wulf's freedom."

"But what does this have to do with Arthur's death? Anything?"

Ella rocked back on her toes and breathed in the sweet jasmine-laden air of the summer garden. "I am unsure. If you didn't gain access to the records room, then I suggest we stick to the plan and go there next. The tenancy agreement might still hold the clue to whoever was putting pressure on Arthur to sell up."

Tomcat's ears dipped. "The town hall was locked up tight. There were lots of extra guards milling around the gates too. I bumped into Cassidy, and I told her what Wulf told you. That Rooster is still being held in Nottingham prison."

Ella narrowed her eyes. "Rooster, I had nearly forgotten about him, but John confirmed it... That was good of you, to let her know. I'm afraid it entirely slipped my mind that she had set me that task..."

Tomcat dropped eye contact and cast a dejected gaze at his little paws. "Yeah, well, if I'm honest, I didn't remind you because it gave me a reason to talk to Cass alone..." He walked back and forth in front of the pond. "That was selfish, and not good teamwork. I guess, I just thought..." He shook his head. "I don't know what I thought... I guess I just wanted to help her, you know, make a difference to her case. Maybe then she'd take me a bit more seriously?"

"Oh, Tom, I understand. Truly, I do. Tonight I found out something about Richard..." Ella trailed off and stared up. Could it be true? All the times Richard had made her feel like she was vital and was valued, and yet in the end he must have just been using her. They were never a team; she was just a cog in whatever he was plotting. "Tom, your talk on teamwork has given me an idea. We should go pay Willow another visit."

"Oh! You think they're *working* together! Willow and Mr Puddles!" Tomcat's tail shot up like a flag. "Why didn't I think of that? It's so obvious!"

"Willow and Mr Puddles? Whatever are you talking about?"

"Hello!" Tomcat gestured, splaying his paws. "I'm a talking cat—maybe Mr Puddles is a talking dog! Maybe he's actually the master-mind behind the whole thing! Willow said a *friend* of Van Helsing used to own Ginger's. Maybe *the friend* got trapped inside Mr Puddles like I was trapped inside Tilly!"

"Magic preserve me, no!" Ella couldn't stop herself from laughing. "Haha! Do you have any idea how much powerful magic that would take! You are a one-in-a-million anomaly. Switching bodies isn't an everyday occurrence!"

"Wulf seems to manage it," Tom muttered sourly, his tail flicking across the colourful mosaic tiles.

"Werewolves can affect a temporary change. *Temporary!*" She sighed and cut off further curt replies before she said something she regretted. "Forgive me, I didn't mean to laugh at you. Of course, you couldn't know how rare you are... I was just contemplating that Willow might still be *partners* with Van Helsing, maybe unwittingly. It's painful to admit, but Richard had me do all sorts of favours for him, and I was none the wiser that he was using me. Even after I lost my wand for misuse of magic... Perhaps whatever Van stole from John, he might have hidden at her property—or across the fence at the Academy."

Tomcat nodded. "That's smart thinking! Maybe I can track it down with my nose!"

"A solid notion. If not, then there's still the records room to access in the town hall."

Tomcat's eyes widened. "We should split up. I'll go check out Willow's, you go research. Hey, here's a thought. Upstairs in the queen's library, does she keep copies of recent newspapers? Maybe if the theft from John was important enough, the *Times* might have reported it."

Ella tapped a hobnail toe on the corridor and hummed to herself. While Tom was clearly trying to keep her out of any danger in his kind but entirely unnecessarily overprotective manner, two could play that game. And while she had him nosing about Willow's, that would leave her free to go back to Arthur's.

If she could just get her hands on the letter from the Nottingham prison informing Arthur of his son's supposed passing, perhaps it might also mention what Wulf had been sentenced for. Even better, it might name his partners in crime...

Chapter 33

The Charmington Werewolf Revealed

Northgate Square, Charmington.

Once Tomcat had scampered off, Ella clutched her stick and braced herself to leave the warmth of the summer garden and face the cold outside. She exited the castle and strode along the covered walkway, grateful for the slight shelter the arched roof provided from the harsh night air.

Really, the nights must be getting colder. Or was she just feeling her age that Sibylla accused her of not acting? Easy for Sibylla to say while tucked up nice and toasty in the heart of their ancient family home...

Ella's thoughts dissipated as, rounding a corner, she spied three children up ahead in distinctive blue and yellow striped jumpers, who were clumped together, whispering. Their furtive attention was focused on the side of the wall where several 'wanted' posters had been pasted.

What were they up to?

"Ho there!" Ella called out, brandishing her walking stick at them.

The children started. One dropped something and shouted, "Leg it!" and they all sprinted off down the alleyway.

The Unikorn Lives! was freshly painted on the stonework in dripping red strokes.

"You don't spell unicorn with a K!" Ella yelled after the laughing children. She stooped to pick up the discarded paintbrush. How easy would it be to correct the spelling? Ella flinched when another figure hurried around the corner and nearly smacked into her. Dirk Turpin, the royal coach driver, his purple frock coat buttoned up tight to his neck. He looked just as surprised to see her.

Ella dropped the brush, and Dirk clutched his coat front that was twitching and bulging out at the stomach. "It's not what it looks like!" they both said at once.

"What are you hiding?" was on Ella's lips when a bark sounded from the depths of Dirk's coat. Up wriggled a little white dog face and peeked out the neckline.

"Mr Puddles," Ella muttered, leaning on her stick. So that's where the unruly little one-eared dog had vanished.

"I couldn't let them hurt him, ma'am!" Dirk blustered, constantly looking behind him as if he was being followed. Mr Puddles wriggled back down into the depths of the warm coat.

"Of course not."

"He's just an innocent little dog. He already lost an ear somehow, and now a bunch of deranged townsfolk want to string him up! It's madness!"

"Quite, madness, I agree..." Ella hummed to herself, "Lost an ear somehow...?" *Was there something in that?* Ella wondered. *One-eared...*

"And, and...oh. Ma'am, you agree with me?" Dirk sagged with relief and leaned against the wall onto the fresh red paint. "Aww! My new coat! If I catch those..." He muttered something under his breath and scrubbed at his ruined sleeve with a silk handkerchief.

Clang! Clang! Clang!

Ella turned towards the sound. The town hall bells. What were they ringing for at this time of night? There must be an emergency.

"Fire!" Dirk said. Forgetting his painted-smeared coat, he balled the ruined handkerchief and stuffed it into a pocket. "Wait here, ma'am, for your own safety. Go back into the castle." He sprinted off down the alley towards Northgate Square and the continuously ringing bells.

"Fire... One-eared dog..." Ella stared at the empty alley down which Dirk had run off. A growing sense of dread flooded her. "Magic preserve!" Ella gasped and smacked her forehead. "One-eared dog! Oh gosh, no! Could that Rooster chap have somehow magically housed his essence within Mr Puddles? No, it *can't* be! The volume of magic it would take to constantly hold that form! No ordinary witch could manage such a feat!"

And grumbling under her breath, she followed after the coachman, as fast as she was able, her stick jabbing at the cobbles. "Oh, if Tom is right, I will *never* live this down!"

She joined the flow of townsfolk who had likewise heard the bells and were also heading to the square, with some carrying buckets, others carrying ropes and pitchforks. Fire or werewolf, they were prepared.

ELLA CAUGHT UP WITH THE three little orphan boys in their matching blue and yellow striped jumpers, who were standing under a streetlamp on the steps outside the haberdashery and pointing across the square to the Gatehouse Inn. Van Helsing stood in the broken window of the dining room that overlooked the square, and he was shouting down to Cassidy and several town guards who were standing below.

"What's going on?" Ella asked the children.

The smallest boy wiped his dripping nose with a well-practised swipe on his jersey sleeve. "Van Smelly done caught the werewolf!"

"Oh no!" Ella gasped. Could Wulf have followed her back into town and been caught? She joined the children in staring up at the unfolding drama.

Behind Ella, a bell tinkled as the shop door opened, and the haberdashery twins ventured out onto their doorstep along with the actress Nigella Pickford, who must have been having a late-night fitting judging from the disarray of her large hat that trailed with ribbons. "Who is it?" the actress enquired in a stage whisper. "I have a bet with Mr Beau."

"Behold!" Van Helsing shouted, and he reached behind him and pulled someone from the shadows of the darkened dining room. "The Charmington werewolf!"

Willow was yanked into view. Tears streamed down her face.

Ella gasped along with everyone else.

Van Helsing shook Willow. "Confess your crimes, foul fiend!" he boomed.

"Yes! Confess!" someone shouted from the crowd, jostling through the guards to get closer under the window. Mistress Fairweather.

Willow knuckled away a tear and mumbled something. A ripple of stillness washed across the people as everyone craned forward, straining to hear what she said.

"Speak up!"

"I am the werewolf," Willow said, louder this time. All the while staring at her feet. Van Helsing gave her another shake, and she hiccupped, and then added, "I killed Arthur."

"You ate her brownies!" Millie wailed, clutching her sister Sally and shaking her. "Willow is a werewolf, and you ate her brownies!"

Sally's eyes rolled back in her head, and she crumpled onto the haberdashery steps. The children regarded the elderly lady with mild curiosity, looking from her lying prone across the shop doorstep over to the sight at the inn, as if wondering which developing performance was going to be more entertaining.

"You two, grab her under her arms," Ella instructed the older children, who shrugged and jumped to the task. "Can you manage her feet?" Ella asked the littlest one, who puffed out his chest and declared, "Two pennies for moving a dead body." And then held out a tiny grubby palm. "Up front."

"She ain't dead," the tallest child replied. While they were arguing how they should structure their fee, Millie's breathing was becoming increasingly erratic. "No! No! She ate the brownies!" Millie barred their entry from the shop and waved them back. "Sally's infected!" And screaming hysterically, Millie slammed the door shut in all their faces.

Nigella Pickford pounded on the door. "This is preposterous. Open this door at once! You can't leave me out here! I'm your best customer!"

"Magic preserve me!" Ella muttered. It was high time someone put a stop to this madness. And as usual, it looked like the job was up to her. Second rule of governing was *if you want something done right, do it yourself.*

Turning on her heel, Ella crossed the square and edged through the crowd. She elbowed through a pair of townsfolk carrying buckets and joined Cassidy and Dirk, who were standing directly below the Gatehouse Inn's broken dining room window.

"Where's my money?" Van Helsing was demanding of the young guardswoman. "I captured your killer. I should be rewarded!"

"And I told you that I don't have the authority," Cassidy was saying in a clear, calm voice, her palms held up and out. "Why don't you let the lady go and come outside?"

"Are you crazy?" Van Helsing snarled, shaking Willow. "Have you *seen* what a werewolf can do?" He kept looking over his shoulder as if expecting the guards to be trying to creep up behind him. His brow was sweating, and his left eye was constantly twitching.

Was he ill? Coming down with something? A touch of insanity, perhaps? Ella wondered as she observed the scene. And the smell. Magic preserve! It was like being hit in the teeth with a hammer. Rancid mutton fat with a hint of something dead.

"I have your fee," Ella called out, wrapping her fingers around Tom's wages-filled letter. She rattled the coins together so he might hear the clink. "The queen has entrusted me to deliver your money on her behalf. With our thanks for your services, of course."

"About time," Mistress Fairweather huffed, crossing her meaty arms. "I pay my taxes, you know!"

Van Helsing clutched Willow tighter as if expecting a trick, but on seeing the guards cede to Ella's authority and let her through, he relaxed a tiny bit.

Cassidy and Dirk exchanged glances, and the coachman began ushering people back. "Show's over, folks, nothing to see, nothing to see."

There were various disappointed grumblings, but people gradually started to move back a few steps. After all, it was late, very cold, and it appeared no one was going to be ripped limb from limb, or anything half so exciting. A hot cup of cocoa was starting to appeal more than standing around for another half hour while slowly losing sensation in one's toes.

Ella drew her cloak tight and regarded Willow standing in the frame of the broken window in the moonlight. Willow's head was bowed, her mussed-up hair falling in her red-rimmed eyes. Was this the face of a terrifying killer?

"I do have one small question," Ella voiced in the crisp night air. "I can't help but notice your *so-called* werewolf is standing in the moonlight, shall we say, a little less hairy than one might expect?" Ella let the accusation hang.

"Aye," Dirk added, with a grin. "Sans beastie, as it were!"

"Ooh, she has you there," Mistress Fairweather chirped, suddenly looking interested in this development.

"What? What?" blustered Van Helsing, drawing the dejected Willow closer to him. "But you heard the creature's full confession!"

"True, but taxpayer money must be spent responsibly." Ella kept her gaze locked on Van Helsing's sweating and trembling face, but from the corner of her eye, she noticed that Cassidy had melted away into the crowd. Was the guardswoman circling around to tackle him from behind?

Van Helsing leaned back into the darkness of the dining room and grabbed something from the nearest table. A butter knife. He pressed it into Willow's side. "Show them. Go on, show them! Howl, wolf!"

Willow flinched, but then threw back her head. "Owww—wah!" Her pathetic howl receded into sobs when beside Ella, Dirk's bulging frock coat front started wriggling and jerking and Mr Puddles' head popped up out from the neckline. The one-eared dog yipped.

"Mr Puddles!" Willow cried joyfully, and then, elbowing Van Helsing in the ribs, she pulled away from him and shouted, "You jerk! You told me Mr Puddles was dead!"

At that moment, Cassidy appeared from the darkness, swept Van Helsing's legs from under him and pinned him to the ground. Her knee pressing into his spine, she said, "I arrest you in the name of the queen for disturbing the peace and for stinking up the place!"

"Fools! You're all fools," shouted Van Helsing, squirming against the guardswoman's hold. He was dragged, cursing and ranting, from view to reappear at the inn's main entrance a minute later as Cassidy hauled him outside down to street level.

Owwww Oooooo!

A howl ripped through the night air.

Everyone froze.

Owwww Oooooo Owww!

Collectively, all heads turned toward the sound. A tall figure clad in a fluttering white garment stood atop the town wall. One moment he was there, the next gone.

"Ghost!" shouted Mistress Fairweather hysterically. "It's the ghost of Arthur!"

"What the...?" Cassidy murmured, taking her eyes off Van Helsing, who stumbled a few steps into the square and tripped over, falling at Ella's feet.

"I told you! I warned you!" Van Helsing growled at Ella and, grabbing her arm, pulled himself to his feet as everyone backed away from them.

"Wolf!" shouted someone, pointing into the dark.

A huge black wolf, trailing a tattered nightgown, launched itself across the cobbles towards the townsfolk.

"Pay him!" Mistress Fairweather shrieked at Ella. "Pay him quick!"

Van Helsing was patting his pockets.

In a split second, Ella looked from Willow clutching Mr Puddles in the ruins of Arthur's dining room, to Van Helsing setting the black pipe to his lips, to the snarling wolf barrelling towards her.

Magic preserve! She was going to die.

Toot—parple—squeak!

Van Helsing blew the pipe as if his life depended on it.

The giant wolf yelped and skidded to a heap at their feet, its black tail brushing across Ella's boots as it writhed in pain.

"Mr Puddles, no!" Willow shouted as the little white dog thrashed in her arms. She couldn't hold him. Snarling, the poodle jumped from the window ledge down onto the cobbles.

—Parple—toot—toot!

The black wolf howled in pain. Ella clutched her ears in sympathy. Oh, it was too cruel, too cruel!

His rat skull necklace jangling, Van Helsing played on, *—squeak— squeak—squeak!*

Mr Puddles approached, lips drawn back, fangs bared, red glowing eyes locked on the writhing, helpless wolf.

Ella gasped. Suddenly, all the pieces fit together. The pipe and the one-eared dog!

"It *was* the dog!" Ella shouted. "*You're* the horrible man that Willow rescued Mr Puddles from. And you *made* Mr Puddles attack Arthur by controlling the dog with magic! Black magic! All because Arthur wouldn't sell up!" It had been staring her in the face all along. The magic flute *and* the dog! That's what Van Helsing had stolen from Prince John.

She struck out. Smacked her open palm against the butt end of the black flute.

Van Helsing gagged as the pipe lodged in his throat. He dropped to one knee.

Ella wrenched the flute free from his windpipe. Cast it on the cobbles and stamped on it with her hobnail boots. Again and again. The bone flute shattered.

And then there was silence.

CHAPTER 34

DUN, DUN, DUNNN!

Van Helsing leaned over and spat blood on the ground. "You stupid old woman, you broke a tooth!"

Mr Puddles, now freed from the evil spell cast by the magic flute, jumped around and yipped like a regular frisky dog, licked Van Helsing's face and then jumped up at Ella's skirts. Wagging his tail, his little pink tongue lolled like this was a fun game, and then he was swept up into Dirk's arms.

Getting to his feet, Wulf, who was once again in human form and half-naked in the remains of Ella's nightgown, placed one hand on Van Helsing's shoulder and announced, "Van Helsing, by order of Prince John, regent of Sherwood, you are under arrest for escaping Nottingham prison, theft, meddling in black magic, and the *most heinous* murder of Arthur, formerly of the Gatehouse Inn, by poodle proxy."

Cassidy looked Wulf up and down, at his broad shoulders straining against the white cotton and the tattered remains of lace about his thighs, and she whistled. "You don't see that every day." She appeared to give herself a mental shake, and was quickly master of the situation once more, gathering the other guards to her. They shackled Van Helsing's wrists behind his back and escorted him away with little resistance.

Perhaps the thought of being imprisoned within a stout lockup, rather than alone in the company of a rogue werewolf, had subdued him. His eye had even stopped twitching by the time he was led away.

As soon as Cassidy and Van Helsing departed, Wulf slumped down onto the frosted steps of his father's café and cradled his head in his hands.

Ella could only imagine the strength and resolve it must have taken for Wulf to let the man who had effectively murdered his father walk away, rather than deal out the swift justice that Ella had no doubt he was capable of delivering, and rip Van Helsing limb from limb with his teeth.

Sometimes, you had to put aside your own desires for the greater good. She cast her eyes across to the children watching from the steps of the haberdashery, and Nigella Pickford directing Mr Beau to assist with convincing Millie to open up and let Sally back inside.

Indeed, sometimes you ended up alone and in the cold, while the world carried on, none the wiser for your sacrifice.

She pulled loose the string on her cloak when Wulf spoke up as if reading her mind. "I don't feel the cold. It's a side effect of the condition, but thank you for your kind thought."

Ella sat down on the step beside him. "Sorry about the bone flute. I take it that and the poodle are what Prince John sent you to retrieve?"

Wulf regarded the smashed-up shards of bone. "I can neither confirm nor deny."

"What about Mr Puddles? Do you really have to take him back?" Ella gestured across the far side of the square to where Mr Puddles was licking Willow's face as she hugged Dirk and thanked him for saving the poodle.

"Mr Puddles, you say?" Wulf cocked an eyebrow and shook his head. "John's dog was called Sir Barksalot...clearly, that must be a different dog entirely..." Self-consciously, he rubbed the silver manacle that was now touching the bare flesh on his wrist. The skin underneath was red and welted.

Ella winced in sympathy. Silver and werewolves did not agree. "The chains that bind," she said softly, more to herself, but Wulf nodded, silently confirming her suspicion that the manacle was what bound Wulf's loyalty to John.

Could Wulf ever be forced to kill on John's command, Ella wondered, just as Mr Puddles had when under the flute's spell?

"Is there a key to your chains?" Ella voiced.

Wulf ran a hand through his tousled hair. "Not in the conventional sense, and maybe not at all... It is a nonsense."

Ella raised an eyebrow. "Go on."

"True love unlocks the manacle." Wulf half-shrugged, as if embarrassed. "Like I said, complete nonsense."

Ella thought back to the looks she had observed Robinne cast over the young man. "I have heard of stranger things... And though I know it's of little consolation, Wulf, your father would have been proud of what you did tonight. He was a man of the law, and revenge is not justice."

"Arthur," Wulf said softly, and Ella was momentarily confused. "You asked what my name is. It's Arthur. After my father."

He looked up, dark eyes thoughtful. So like Arthur's. How was it she had never noticed?

"I am pleased to know you, Arthur. And if I might request a favour, I have a letter I need to be delivered in Nottingham." She felt in her pocket for Tom's letter to the Nottingham home for unwanted boys. "Do you know of this orphanage?"

Wulf nodded. "I do, and it would be my pleasure." He narrowed his eyes. "But there's something else, isn't there? Ask it."

"My lodger Tom April grew up at this boys' home. Poor lad, he knows nothing of his family. I was hoping, with your position, you might be able to make a few *discreet* enquiries as to how Tom came to be there."

Wulf rubbed his face and frowned. "I'm not sure that would be advisable. This orphanage has something of a reputation. A place where rich and powerful men dump unwanted complications. You understand me?" He fixed her with a stern look. "Powerful men don't like their past to come calling."

Ella blinked. "I hear you. Forget I asked. I would not wish to put you, or Tom, in any danger."

But Wulf shrugged and took the envelope. "Huh. What's a little danger to a werewolf?"

Ella nodded. "Then I will trust your discretion in that matter. And whenever you are in Wyld Enchantment Woods again, you are always welcome at my cottage. You might be interested to know that Robinne is a frequent visitor, also. I'm sure the two of you would find a lot in common to discuss." She cast a regret-filled look at the remains of what had been her favourite lace nightgown. "And should you find yourself caught, shall we say, indisposed, and I am not at home, from now on I shall always ensure a fresh shirt is left out in my barn."

"And pants," muttered Wulf—Arthur—managing a wry smile. "If I may intrude on your kindness once more. This job is tough on pants."

CHAPTER 35

HOME AGAIN, HOME AGAIN.

Riverside Cottage, Wyld Enchantment Woods, the next day.

"And then what happened?" asked Robinne, while tending the wood stove in Ella's kitchen the next morning.

"So, naturally, I amended my offer. A clean shirt *and* trousers," Ella laughed from her perch at the table. "Then who should come along? Tom trots up, brownie crumbs all over his whiskers! Tom takes one look at the now-deserted square and says, 'Did I miss anything?'" Ella rocked back on the chair and mimed brushing her face. "You should have seen him. His face, all covered in brownie crumbs!"

"That's not quite how I remember it," Tom huffed from his position on top of the pine table. "And it was cocoa powder, not brownie! I told you I fell in the cocoa bag when I squeezed in Willow's bakery window." He crossed his paws tightly across his tummy. "Could have happened to anyone."

"Oh, of course, of course," Ella teased, as Robinne carried over a steaming saucepan of water and sloshed it into a mixing bowl in which Ella had already placed a handful of dried black currants. "Right, let's try this, shall we?" Ella smoothed out a recent copy of the *Nottingham Times* atop the table and dunked a rag into the hot water.

"But Willow used blueberries..." Tomcat said, peering close as the water flooded across the newsprint.

"I suspect that was just for a colourant, not for any magical chemical," Ella said, dabbing the rag over the main headline that read

| *Paper worth more than gold?*

All three stared as the newsprint remained stubbornly static.

After a minute, Ella dusted her hands. "Oh well, I guess sometimes news is just news."

"Um... Do you think it's maybe, just maybe, because your magical powers have been bound?" Tomcat touched his paws together as if he were afraid to even bring up the painful reminder.

Ella shrugged. "Perhaps. Though it's true my academic magic is bound, I thought my natural wyld magic would suffice."

"You said Willow showed you this, right?" Robinne added, also not quite meeting Ella's gaze. "She's not from here, so she can't have wyld magic, so I have to agree with Tom..."

Ella sighed. Two against one. Fine. "A fair point. Let it be said, I'm not too proud to admit when I'm wrong."

Ella's mind darted to thoughts from last night—imagine if Mr Puddles had been the smuggler Rooster chap in some magical disguise. Ha! Thank goodness that hadn't been true!

No doubt, she would never even set eyes on the rogue. He'd be foolish to come back to Charmington after he had set Gretel's business on fire—Gretel would not take kindly to his return.

Robinne stood up from the table. "Right, I'm on pancake duty. All this talk of blueberries has made me hungry."

Ella sat back as Tomcat likewise bounded off the table, and the pair of them set about to prepare breakfast. She let out a small smile of satisfaction as the youngsters bustled around her kitchen and cast her gaze upon the cottage she loved, glancing outside at the chickens pecking the dirt. A curious pumpkin vine was winding the handle of the water well, lowering and then raising the well's bucket.

Maybe Richard had *coerced* and used her magic for his own purposes to build this little cottage but she could never regret the home she had created. She loved this place and these people. She relaxed and half-listened as Tomcat debated the virtues of using syrup over sugar grains.

Her eyes drifted once more to the soaked newspaper.

> *Paper worth more than gold?*
>
> *In the coming months, Nottingham will be trialling paper currency. Our reporters went out on the street to gauge popular opinion and ask—what can go wrong?*

"Paper currency? What a foolish notion! Why, it could be burned in a fire, for one thing!" Ella tutted aloud.

"They use it in Avalon, remember, Cassidy said," Tomcat said over his shoulder as he supervised Robinne in stirring the pancake mixture.

"A modern marvel, apparently," added Robinne, while splashing vanilla into the batter.

Ella rolled her eyes. "Avalon! That explains it. It's probably one of Merlin's outlandish ideas. You won't see me embroiled in such a scheme. Mark my words. Wyld kingdom will adopt paper money over my dead body!"

~ The End ~

Quick, turn the page to learn what's

in store for Ella and Tom

In Book 3 in the Series:

ACE POST MORTEM TWIST

BOOK 3 IN THE SERIES
'ACE POST MORTEM TWIST'

Is Cassidy Turpin a crooked cop?

When Tomcat's secret crush is arrested for murdering a co-worker, Ella and Tom only have 24 hours to clear Cassidy's name before she is shipped off to the notorious Nottingham prison.

But with Tomcat determined to call the shots, will the cat save the day or trip up Ella's every step?

Post Mortem **Book 3 in the Wyld Enchantment Woods Cozy Mystery series – out soon!**

Follow my Amazon author page to stay up to date with all titles in the series.
https://www.amazon.com/stores/Kura-Jane-Carpenter/author/B0BGT43WSR

Acknowledgements

I am especially indebted to my lovely beta readers, **Kay Mercer** and **Angela Oliver**, whose feedback was once again invaluable.

Plus, a special shout out and 'welcome to the beta reader team, sister dear, **Alice Carpenter**'. I'm very glad to have you aboard.

In addition, I would like to offer my heartfelt thanks to the kind *ARC Readers* of this novel and book 1, *Mirror Mirror, Who's the Killer?* Your reviews are truly appreciated!

Finally, many thanks to **Kevin Berry** for proofreading.

About the Author

Kura Jane Carpenter is a New Zealand author and was the 2019 recipient of the Sir Julius Vogel award for Best New Talent.
When not writing, Kura enjoys convincing strangers that greyhounds make the best pets.

Web: **www.kuracarpenter.com**

Instagram: @kura.carpenter

BookBub: https://www.bookbub.com/authors/kura-jane-carpenter

Amazon Author Profile: https://www.amazon.com/stores/Kura-Jane-Carpenter/author/B0BGT43WSR

Link Tree: https://linktr.ee/kurajane

Other Books in the Wyld Enchantment Woods Series

Book 1

Mirror Mirror, Who's the Killer?

Who has silenced the magic mirror?

Ella Charming is a suspended fairy godmother trying to keep her head down in the frozen kingdom of Wyld Enchantment Woods where magic is strictly forbidden.

When a henchman turns up on her doorstep with a stolen magic mirror in his pocket and an arrow lodged in his heart, Ella is forced to get involved.

With only the aid of a tattletale talking cat who works for the wicked queen, can Ella find the murderer before she is blamed for theft or worse—magic?